HOME ACROSS THE ROAD

a novel

by Nancy Peacock

LONGSTREET
Atlanta, Georgia

The White Redds

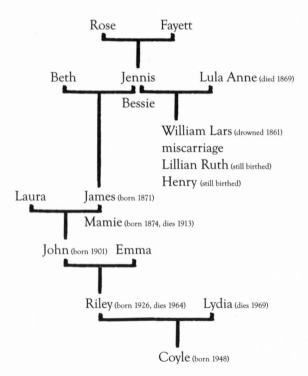

Rose — Fayett

Beth — Jennis — Lula Anne (died 1869)

Bessie

William Lars (drowned 1861)
miscarriage
Lillian Ruth (still birthed)
Henry (still birthed)

Laura — James (born 1871)

Mamie (born 1874, dies 1913)

John (born 1901) — Emma

Riley (born 1926, dies 1964) — Lydia (dies 1969)

Coyle (born 1948)

The Black Redds

Jennis Redd   Cally   Tom

Cleavis   Tuly, Jed, Abe   Maude

Earnestine   Joe, Alfie (dies 1912)

China (born 1912)   Amzie Washington

Earnest   Julia

Leon Jordan   Abolene

Cally (born 1971)

For Momma

Special thanks to members of my writers' group,
Virginia Holman, Marjorie Hudson, and Tony Peacock.
Also to Lee Glenn for giving me a computer when mine
broke down, Ben Campbell for giving me emotional sup-
port when I broke down, John Yow and Sally McMillan
for being in the ring with me.

Published by
LONGSTREET, INC.
A subsidiary of Cox Newspapers
A subsidiary of Cox Enterprises, Inc.
2140 Newmarket Parkway
Suite 122
Marietta, GA 30067
www.lspress.com

Copyright © 1999 by Nancy Peacock

All rights reserved. No part of this book may be reproduced in any form or by any means
without the prior written permission of the Publisher, excepting brief quotations used in
connection with reviews, written specifically for inclusion in a magazine or newspaper.

Printed in the United States of America

1st printing 1999

Library of Congress Catalog Card Number: 99-61756

ISBN: 1-56352-509-7

Jacket design by Paulette Livers Lambert
Book design by Megan Wilson

HOME ACROSS THE ROAD

"THE UNIVERSE IS MADE OF STORIES, NOT ATOMS."

— Muriel Rukeyser

China

1

In 1971, China Redd was waiting to die. She was sixty-one years old and her eyes were rheumy and clouded and her back was bent and frail. Her hands shook and her breath felt shallow, like it wasn't getting down into her body, like it wasn't going to all the places that a breath is supposed to go.

Her granddaughter, Abolene, told her that she wasn't sick. The doctor put the cold round disc of the stethoscope against the bones of China's thin, brown chest and declared her healthy as a hog.

Young, both of them. What would they know about dying or about the tiredness she felt in her bones and her soul?

Only China Redd knew how it felt to be inside her body and she had spent sixty-one years inside that body, forty-seven of them asking hardly anything but work out of it, asking nothing but work from her hands and her bones and her back and her arms.

The work began in 1926, on the day she turned fourteen, when China Redd followed her mother down the narrow dirt-packed track leading from their home and into the oak-lined driveway of the home across the road.

China Redd was tall enough, even then, to reach the key that hung off a string from the new light fixture on the back porch of the big house called Roseberry. She slipped the key into the lock, turned the knob and stepped into the dark kitchen. China could feel its space all around her and her mother picked up her hand and guided it along the wall, showing her the push-button switch that flooded the kitchen with modern electric light.

At age fourteen China started working for the white Redds in the big old house called Roseberry. At age fourteen China Redd began a lifetime of mornings spent cracking eggs into a bowl and brewing coffee and spreading softened butter across bread that was toasted the color of her skin.

For forty-seven years China slid a key into a lock and let herself into a back door. She scrubbed Roseberry's floors and polished its silver and watched its babies grow up and leave home. She rinsed out washtubs and bathtubs and cooked and folded laundry and swept and vacuumed. She had seen its weddings and its showers, its wakes and its funerals. She had seen its bridge games and Christmas parties and Easter dinners. She had fed and bathed and wiped the noses of children that were never her own and now, as China Redd waited to die, the big old house called Roseberry stood as empty as she felt herself to be.

Windows were broken out and doors left ajar. Floors that China had shined were now scuffed and dulled with films of dust and dirt. Names of teenagers were spray painted across cracked plaster walls. Dishes were broken and scattered across the cracked gray linoleum of the kitchen floor, and sitting in an open cabinet was a fluted, white bowl with a bird's nest cupped inside.

In the dining room of Roseberry, a wisteria vine had broken through the window and twined itself around the very table legs that China had crawled on her hands and knees to polish. It wound itself around chairs and crawled across the mahogany table, and trapped inside its jungle were the dishes of Coyle Redd's last meal, still crusted with food that China had cooked.

It seemed to China that nothing she had ever done mattered anymore, if it had ever mattered at all. Not one pan that had been carefully washed, not one stain gotten out of a white linen shirt, not one wrinkle ironed out of slacks or sheets—none of it mattered now.

Children grew up and went away, sometimes forever, sometimes to places unknown, sometimes for reasons that could never be understood. No doubt Abolene would be leaving soon, leaving and taking China's great-grandbaby and all the life of the house with her. Soon China's house would be left as empty as Roseberry was left on the day that Coyle Redd died.

Coyle Redd was the last of the white Redds and he was gone forever now. He was gone and China's own son, Earnest, had vanished one day sixteen years earlier and there wasn't any reason to hope any more that he would come home. China was tired of waiting for him but she didn't know anything else.

China didn't know anything else but waiting. All her life she had waited on the needs of the white Redds. When Earnest was a child she had waited on his stuttering words to form a sentence. When he had disappeared she had waited for him to come home but there was no point in that now, so instead she waited to die.

She would wake up in the mornings and creak her legs over the edge of the bed, testing the floor with her feet. If the soles of China's feet felt the hard braid of the rug, then China knew it was another day and she asked God how much longer.

"How much longer?" she would say as she crept down the hallway and into the bathroom and eased herself down onto the toilet. "How much longer?" she would say as she sat in a rickety white chair at the kitchen table and nibbled a few bites of the breakfast that Abolene cooked for her. "How much longer?" China would ask as she pushed the plate away.

In 1971, Abolene was seventeen years old and the spitting image of her father. She was tall and strong with thick, heavy veins roping across the backs of her hands. She had Earnest's almond-colored skin. She had his deep-set eyes. She had thin, elegant fingers, the same as China remembered Earnest's to be. Abolene even had the same cocky walk as Earnest, the same prideful stride that had so often gotten him into trouble with the white men in town. China couldn't help but think of Earnest when she looked at Abolene.

Every morning Abolene set a cup of hot black coffee in front of her grandmother and asked, "Is today the day?"

"I don't think so," China would say. "I don't think He's going to take me today. Maybe tomorrow."

Waiting to die was slow work. There was nothing to do

to speed up the process. Nothing that China wanted to do, anyway. So she waited and she thought and she remembered.

After breakfast China Redd would move from the kitchen to the front room where she would slowly sink into the couch. She would shift from side to side, trying to get away from the broken spring that poked its way through the scratchy blue upholstery. If she could see through the window that the weather was nice, China would pull herself up from the couch and shuffle to the porch. She would sit in the old La-Z-Boy recliner and tug at her housedress, lifting first one cheek and then the other, finally nodding to Abolene who would raise the lever that kicked out the little shelf for China's feet. Abolene would drape an old yellow blanket across her grandmother. She would tuck the edges in around China's spindly legs. She would ask, "Is it okay?"

China nodded.

A few minutes later Abolene would come out on the porch again, wearing her brown K&W Cafeteria uniform and her white nurse's shoes.

"Okay?" she would ask again

China would nod.

"Give Great-granny a kiss," Abolene would say to her ten-month-old daughter, and China would feel the infant's sticky lips against her too-soft cheek. She would watch them drive away together in the old dented Valiant that Abolene had bought with her own money.

The car would dust along the driveway and then turn onto the road. The tires would swoosh along the pavement and soon even the engine couldn't be heard and it was quiet and it was just China sitting on the porch in the old La-Z-Boy recliner.

She gazed across the field in front of her. China stared beyond the cows that were grazing there. Her eyes went past the dew-covered spiderwebs that were spread across the grass every morning, like a thousand tossed handkerchiefs gleaming in the bright, early light. Her gaze went over the two-lane blacktop, past the chain that blocked the entrance, along the oak trees and the rutted driveway and the weed-choked walkway and up the old gray steps to the porch of Roseberry.

There was no one left alive that knew Roseberry like China Redd. She could recall seeing that house painted white with gray shutters one year and gray with white shutters another. China could recall seeing that house painted in just about every kind of way and she could recall seeing that house with no paint at all when she was a little girl and Roseberry stood across the road, rustic and brown and weather-worn, just like her own little house, just as rustic and brown and weather worn as it was now.

There were lots of stories about Roseberry, none of them true as far as China could tell. Those stories circulated the town and the county like the ghosts that they were. Those stories were published, published like they were real, published in a book called *The Legends of Roseberry*, written by a woman named Lydia Redd, one of the white women that China had worked for during her life.

When the book was published, it had been China who had served at the party Lydia Redd threw for herself. It was 1965, the year before Abolene's mother died. The year before twelve-year-old Abolene left her home in Wake County to come and live with China in Chatham.

China remembers clearly standing in the kitchen of Roseberry, arranging celery sticks and slices of cheese and carrot strips across a glass platter. She remembers clearly hearing the squeak of the swinging door behind her as one of the guests pushed his way through. She remembers the footsteps and the soft pad of shoe leather on linoleum and the way that he came to lean against the counter beside her.

"Mrs. Redd tells me that you're descended from the slaves that worked this plantation," he said. He picked up a piece of celery and crunched down on it. "Is that true?"

"That's true," China said but that was all she would say. In 1965, China Redd didn't want to talk and even if she had wanted to talk she wouldn't have expected to be heard.

China Redd had stories inside of her, stories that clawed at her throat like an untreated virus, stories that would probably never see the pages of a book, but books were not what made things true.

China Redd knew that her stories were true. She knew it from the earrings that she had in her own possession, and if that wasn't enough, there was a picture inside of Lydia Redd's book of those very same earrings, earrings that China's great-grandmother had stolen from the white Redds.

China's great-grandmother was born in a small cabin behind the big house called Roseberry. China's great-grandmother was a woman named Cally, born with brown skin and blue eyes. But those eyes were not blue on the day that she was buried.

If someone had asked how such a thing was possible, China would have told the truth. She would have said it is only grief that can change the color of a woman's eyes.

Cally

2

Cally was born with blue eyes, daughter of both black and white, but white didn't claim her, except as property. Born a slave to a slave mother, Cally became a slave herself and when she was big enough she hauled water to the big house for cooking and cleaning. She hauled water to the laundress where a fire was roaring and spitting and clothes were bubbling in a big iron pot. She hauled water to the stables and filled the troughs. She hauled water to the overseer in the field and finally she was allowed to carry a bucket down the rows of cotton and give a dipperful to each field hand, her momma being one of them and the man her momma was married to.

When Cally was big enough she lined up before sunrise with the rest of them and she took the hoe in her hand and followed them out into the fields where she chopped cotton and trailed behind the plow, picking up rocks. There were never more rocks than in Chatham County and the field hands wondered that there were fields at all in such a place.

But there were fields and they were created by them and those that went before them and Cally spent all her life in one, except for Sundays and a few days around the time her babies were born.

She got married to a man named Tom. He said he was her husband and she believed him, even though they both knew either of them might be sold away and then there might be another wife or another husband. There was nothing to be done for that but pray.

And pray Cally did. Every night and every day. Every rock picked up and tossed into the back of a wagon was a prayer. Every weed pulled was a prayer. The feel of the rough wooden-handled hoe was a prayer that got offered down every row, in every field, beside every well-tended plant. Cally prayed the hardest after Tom moved into the cabin with her. She prayed that Master Redd would stop his visiting but he didn't.

He still came around, knocking on the door and sending Tom away for something and stepping inside with a cold smirk on his face. Cally would close her own blue eyes and pray to make it quick and when Tom came back to the cabin, there wouldn't be a word said between them. He would pull the old hickory stump up close to the fire and poke at a log with his foot and sparks would go flying up the chimney.

This alone could have been enough to change the color of a woman's eyes, but Cally's eyes didn't turn until after her first live child was born.

There was no telling whose babies the first two were. They both miscarried early on but it was easy to tell that the third one wasn't Tom's. All the same Tom took it up in his arms and said, "You're more mine than his."

They named the baby Cleavis, after Tom's granddaddy, a man who got too old to work and was said by the white folks to be staying alive just for spite.

Cally was hurting from childbirth. Her insides felt like they had been ripped out, but it was spring and there was work to do. Cally wrapped the cloths between her legs to catch the blood. She got up early in the morning and followed her husband out into the fields and the second most beautiful thing she saw that day was the sunrise splaying its pink fingers across the sky.

The first most beautiful thing she saw was her baby and come noontime Cally rushed back to the hut where Miss Liza kept the children and she nursed Cleavis as long as she could and the white man recorded the name of the newborn in a leather-bound journal. "Cleavis. Born to Cally. April, 1855."

The white man was named Jennis Redd and he had a wife and a baby too. The wife's name was Lula Anne and the baby's name was William Lars Redd and he and Cleavis grew up playing together. In 1861, they were both six years old and it had been Cleavis's job to haul water for over a year now, just like it had been Cally's when she was his age.

One day Cleavis was drawing the bucket up from the well. He was trying to hurry because this was the trip to the fields for the hands and his momma was pregnant and Cleavis wanted to bring her water. It was hot for May and his momma needed water. He was pulling on the ropes and trying to blow a fly out of his face when he heard William Lars Redd saying, "I got something to show you."

Cleavis set the bucket on the edge of the well and watched as William opened his palm to show his friend the earrings that he had stolen from his momma. They were not like anything that Cleavis had ever seen. They had swirls of color in them, blues and greens and grays, and William Lars Redd said, "It's a shell called abolene. Here, you can hold them."

Cleavis wiped his hands on his pants and held out one palm and William laid the earrings there like they were tiny robin's eggs and might break at the slightest pressure. Cleavis ran his finger along the teardrops of swirls and they were as slick and smooth as the glass in the windows of the big house that he had snuck up one time and touched. Cleavis pinched the earrings and let them dangle in the sunlight. "Abolene," he repeated.

It was right then that Lula Anne stepped out the back door and saw her son playing with the little black boy again and saw her own earrings in the hands of that boy and saw for the thousandth time that the features of that boy resembled those of her own husband. That thieving boy. Lula Anne had him sold and William Lars Redd didn't say a thing.

Jennis Redd wasn't there. He was gone to Wake County. Gone to talk to important men about a new government for the South, gone so far away that he couldn't argue that Cleavis was going to grow up to be a strong field hand and it didn't make sense to go selling him now.

Jennis Redd was gone for a week and the slave trader came by the very next day and hauled Cleavis off in a wagon and it was the last that Cally ever saw of her boy.

When he didn't bring the water that day she knew that something was wrong and she prayed and kept on pounding her hoe against the dusty Chatham County dirt. The only sounds were the hard thumping of fifty hoes against the earth and the whinny of the overseer's horse and Cally knew and Tom knew that something had happened to their boy.

He was locked in the barn and she was allowed to visit him that night and he cried and leaned against her. He knew the word "sold." He'd seen the slave trader come through with a wagon-load of black people, shackled and chained and wondering where they were going and would they see their families again.

Cleavis told his momma about the earrings called abolene. "I didn't steal them," he said. "I didn't steal them. How could I? I'm not allowed inside the big house."

Cally held her boy's head against the round of her belly. She didn't lie to him. She said it plain as day and then choked down crying. "I may never see you again," she said.

There were no words of comfort, nothing in a mother's heart to prepare her for this, even though all her life she knew that this might be the very thing that could happen.

"Pray," was all that Cally could tell him. "You got to pray every day," she said. "You got to pray with all your heart. Promise me you will."

Cleavis nodded, tears running down his cheeks, and there was a knock on the door and the overseer stepped in and dragged Cally out of the barn and, working in the fields the next day, she sobbed and chopped and listened for the rattle of the wagon that would take her boy away.

After three weeks of crying and hoeing Cally felt like she couldn't cry anymore and she got quiet. Tom begged her, "Talk to me, Honey. Just talk to me."

But Cally wouldn't talk. She lay her hands on her belly,

five months along now, and she shook her head from side to side and she hated white folks so bad right then that she willed the white blood right out of her and changed the color of her eyes from blue to slate gray.

Tom saw it and by the firelight he rubbed his thumbs across her eyelids and then held her close to him and said, "You talk when you're ready, Cally. I ain't going nowhere."

Cally wasn't ready for another month, and the cabin was quiet every night. The only light was by the moon and the stars because it was summer now and there was no need of a fire. Lying beside her husband in their dark cabin one night, a whippoorwill calling at the edge of the fields they worked by day, Cally suddenly broke her quiet and said, "I want those earrings."

Tom sighed. He reached over and grabbed his wife's hand and said, "I can't get you those earrings, Darling."

Cally stayed on her back, looking up at the moon shining through a crack in the ceiling and she said, "If I'm going to lose my boy to a pair of earrings, then I am damn well going to have those earrings."

Cally lay her hand on her husband's chest and felt his breath. She felt him sigh again and Tom sighed so big and so heavy this time that his breath leaked out of the drafty cabin and crossed the fields of cotton and circled Roseberry like wind. Tom's sigh caused a chill all across Chatham County and the white folks inside the big house rubbed their hands across their arms and called for the servants to close the shutters. And even so, Tom's sigh was a bitter wind that they could not keep out. Tom's sigh was a coldness that crept inside their bones.

3

Cally got those earrings. Got them one moonless Carolina night and hid them in the crevice of a rock piling at the corner of her house.

It wasn't one month later that William Lars Redd died, slipping off a rock and falling into the rushing brown waters of the Haw River. His body swept downstream for two miles before it caught on a logjam and was discovered by three girls fishing.

Two years after that Lula Anne miscarried again and in 1865 she still-birthed out in the woods, hiding out there in the jungles of wisteria and poison ivy for fear of Sherman's troops advancing.

After Cally took possession of the earrings, Lula Anne had terrible luck with her children and in 1869 she still-birthed once more, finally dying herself this time and leaving Jennis with the chance to marry a woman named Beth, who gave him two live children.

So it was not the end of the white Redds after Cally took possession of the earrings, but Cally thought for a while that it might be and Cally and Tom knew it was the earrings that cursed the white folks and kept their own babies safe.

After Cally took possession of the earrings, not one baby was sold or died or took sick and one, the boy named Abe, was even born a free child, by law.

But there was no law the night that Cally got those earrings. No law for a woman born with brown skin and blue eyes. On the night that Cally got the earrings there was only prayer and a moonless sky.

It was July. Cleavis had been gone for two months now and Cally was getting bigger and bigger with the baby inside of her and she put one hand on the small of her back and lowered herself carefully to the split-log step outside her cabin and waited. The air was thick as weeds, as dark and hot and still as stagnant waters. The bugs were biting hard, but Cally did not dare slap at them and they covered her arms with fierce little stings and Cally thought to herself that everything wanted a piece of her flesh.

Cally waited and waited and finally a man slipped out of the shadows with an old feed sack wrapped around his face. He appeared silently, as quiet as a ghost and reached for her hand and opened her palm and lay the teardrop-shaped earrings there, against her skin. Without a word Cally closed her hand around them and the man disappeared.

Cally pulled from the pocket of her dress a boll of cotton snitched from the gin house and a tiny bit of worn cloth torn from her own head rag. She wrapped the earrings inside these things and crept to the back of her cabin. She hid the earrings there, shoving them deep into the crevice of a corner piling and wiping her hands on her dress.

Cally remembered the last time she had seen Cleavis. She remembered the way his head felt against her belly, the soft nub of his hair, the tears he cried that soaked into her dress and her skin and her heart. Cally remembered the word he had said for the earrings. Abolene. "It was a shell called abolene," he said.

Cally ran her hands along the bigness of her belly. Inside there was a fluttering.

She didn't tell Tom. She didn't have to. Tom knew Cally well and from the moment she mentioned the earrings, he knew she would get them just as surely as she had gotten him.

He knew the night it happened, heard the brief rustle of grass as Cally knelt at the back of the cabin, knew it for sure the minute she slipped back inside and lay down beside him. Tom didn't say anything. He just placed the flat of his palm against her belly and waited for a movement that didn't come.

"Is it alright?" he asked.

"I think so," Cally said. "I felt it just now."

The cabins were searched a few days later. They were all lined up outside one morning, long before daybreak, long before the time of day when they were herded out into the fields for work. It was the overseer and two other men that rousted them out of their sleep and lined them up outside and searched every cabin, their lanterns swinging wildly as they turned over bedding and threw what few possessions anyone had out onto the hard-packed Chatham County earth.

There was not one slave at Roseberry Plantation who did not know who had the earrings and where and why. But even so, even with the threat of whipping, no one told and no one grumbled as they were sent in a straight-lined row off to the fields two hours earlier than usual.

The earrings stayed in the crevice of the corner piling and a war started and William Lars Redd slipped off that rock and drowned and one month and seven nights after that, Cally gave birth to a baby girl.

She was big and healthy with a head full of dark hair and they named her Tuly. She looked just like Tom and so did the next one, named Jed, and the one after that, named Abe—the one who was born just five weeks after Jennis Redd called all the field hands up to the big house and said they were free now.

"What should we do?" someone asked.

"Get back to work," Jennis growled.

He went inside and shut the door. They could hear Lula Anne weeping through the open window.

There was murmuring among themselves. Some of the young folks whooped and hollered. Some of the older folks went back to the fields and started hoeing again. Some folks wandered off and were never seen again.

Cally and Tom walked away towards their cabin, Cally big with her baby and waddling along and Tom walking next to her, carrying the baby Jed in one arm and holding little Tuly's hand. They went inside the cabin and shut the door and Tom and Cally sat on the hickory stumps and wondered what to do.

"We got to stay here," Cally answered. "He might come home."

"Who might come home?" Tuly asked.

"Cleavis," Tom answered. "Your brother Cleavis. He might come home."

But he never did and the earrings stayed tucked into the crevice of those rocks for fifty-one years and it was China's father, Joe, who finally moved them.

During all those years Cally had taken them out of their hiding place four times, once each to show them to her children and tell them the story of Cleavis, and again in secret to hold them up to her own ears and wonder what it would be like to wear such a pretty thing.

Tom caught her doing this. He came around the corner of the cabin and seeing the earrings out in the light of day, he rushed up and snatched them out of her hands. "You ought not to be doing that," he said.

Cally near about jumped a mile high and she turned on him and said, "You ought not to sneak up on a gal like that."

"You ought not to have them out in the light," Tom repeated. "Here, I got this," he said. He showed her the thin tin snuffbox in his hand. "I thought we could put them in this," he said. "They'll stay safer and darker."

Tom twisted the top off. He handed the earrings back to Cally and told her to wrap them up and she nestled them into the cotton and wrapped the cloth into a tight little bundle and dropped them in. Tom closed the lid and knelt down and reached his hand under the house. He felt with his fingers along the rough rocks of the corner piling. When he drew his hand out the snuffbox was gone.

"Those earrings weren't ever meant to see the light of day," he said.

China

4

This was the story that China Redd had heard all her life. She had heard it by the dim light of kerosene lamps. She had heard it beside tubs of heated water with washboards propped inside. She had heard it between the rows of corn and beans and sweet potatoes that her father grew in the scruff of dirt out back.

China had heard about Cally and Tom and Cleavis. She had heard about Tom's bone-chilling sigh and she had touched cloth that had been wrapped around Cally's head on the day her son was sold away. China knew how the earrings came to be kept under the house. China knew how they had been passed from Cally to Abe and how Abe had given them to Maude as a wedding present. China knew how Maude had put them back under the house on the day her first child died.

China knew how Maude had crawled out of bed, still bleeding from childbirth and how her legs had shook like tiny branches in a wind when she stood. China knew how Maude had taken the snuffbox off the mantel and stumbled outside with it and tucked it into the crevice of the corner piling once again. China knew how Abe found her there, fainted with blood between her legs and dirt on her cheek and how he'd cried and carried her back to bed and told her he was sorry. He'd find her another wedding present, he said, and Maude told him, "Anything. Anything but those earrings."

China grew up knowing about those earrings, about Cally and Tom and Cleavis, about Maude and Abe and about the day her own father moved them from the cabin to their new home across the road. The earrings were moved on the very day that China Redd was born and China's birth inside their new house was as much a part of the story as Cally's cloth and the cotton snitched from the gin house.

China Redd was born on the kitchen floor of their new house, a new house built on land that was bought from the white Redds, bought with hard-earned money saved by generations and kept stuffed in the upholstery of an old discarded chair.

On the day that they moved, Joe Redd packed the snuffbox deep into a bundle of quilts and clothes. He tucked this bundle under one arm, propped the Bible and a cast-iron frying pan on top and rested the hand of his other arm against the small of his pregnant wife's back.

It was fall and the leaves were turning. The hill behind the row of cabins was dotted with the flaming red and gold of maples. Joe's and Earnestine's feet scuffed loudly through the brown oak leaves that covered the driveway of Roseberry.

Not one person saw them off. Not one white person stepped out onto the porch of Roseberry and smiled or waved or even watched as the last of the black Redds left the land that they had worked but never owned. Not one black person stepped from the darkness of a crumbling cabin to stand in the stoop and wish them well.

Joe and Earnestine were the last people living in that row of cabins and Joe had been born there and he had spent his entire life watching folks leave or die until the cabins echoed empty, all but one.

A family of foxes moved into the last cabin. It was the one closest to the woods, the one that had belonged to Miss Liza in the old days, the woman who kept the children while the slaves worked out in the hot fields. It was the cabin that Cally had rushed towards to nurse her babies, the white overseer sitting high on his horse and laughing as she practically pulled her dress open as she ran, the milk there leaking out of her nipples and hurting her breasts and falling to the ground and Cally knowing it was milk that her babies needed.

Cally and Tom and Tuly were buried up on the hill in a clearing marked with rocks. Jed had left, but Abe stayed on and married the girl named Maude and after her first baby died, there were two more. Two sons named Joe and Alfie and it was Joe and Alfie who managed to buy the small tract of scruffy land from the white Redds.

The land sat right across the dirt road from Roseberry and it was as useless and full of rocks as the fields behind Roseberry had once been. Joe and Alfie set to work, building a small frame house on it, the first task being the building of six foundation pilings, the rocks laid just so in one of them, creating a crevice just large enough to hide the earrings in.

Joe and Alfie scrounged materials and cut corners and worked on Sundays, which was the only day off from the work that they did at Roseberry. It took a year to build, but finally it was done and just as Joe was hammering the last nail into the tin roof, Alfie stood up and whooped and threw his hammer in the air and slipped and fell.

Joe stood on the roof, watching his brother tumble and hearing the tin crumpling beneath his weight. When Alfie hit the ground, Joe could tell by the crunching sound and the silence that followed that Alfie had broken his neck and wouldn't be living there with him and his new wife and the baby that would be born soon.

The earrings looked after the children but they couldn't help a grown-up man. That was how Joe believed it to be, and he buried Alfie in the cemetery behind Mt. Zion Baptist Church and they moved into the new house the very next day.

Earnestine went into labor pains along the way. It was right beside the kitchen house that the first one hit. Close to the well where Cleavis had drawn water that the second one hit. Just in front of the dining room window of Roseberry that the third one hit. Earnestine bent over double with each one of them.

"This baby's coming today, Joe," Earnestine said. "I can feel it. Lord have mercy, I can feel it."

They hurried on, every few feet Earnestine groaning and stopping and clutching her stomach and Joe pulling on her arm and saying, "Come on, now. We got to get them put away."

Joe meant the earrings. He shifted his eyes from side to

side. He lowered his voice, scared that one of the white Redds might come out of the house and say, "I knew you had them all along. Thieves, every one of you. No-good thieves. Now give them back."

Joe tucked the bundle of clothes and quilts tighter under his arm and tried to push his wife along the road.

Earnestine bent double in the middle of the driveway, again at the mailbox, three times along the fence line that separated good land from their land and once more stepping up onto the porch of their new house.

When they got inside Earnestine lay down on the kitchen floor with her knees in the air and just as China's head was crowning, Joe was scurrying outside to hide the earrings. Just as China slid out of her mother's womb onto the hard-planked floor, Joe was shoving the snuffbox of earrings into a crevice in the corner piling, and just as Earnestine was clearing the baby's face and nose, Joe was standing back up and swiping the dirt from the knees of his overalls. When he opened the back door to their new home, the first sound he heard was the squalling of a new baby girl named China.

Sometimes it felt to China that she was born to be in a kitchen. She had spent plenty of her life standing on the faded, brown blood stain on the kitchen floor, standing on the very spot she had first hit when she was born, standing there and scrambling eggs or frying bacon or making coffee or washing dishes. She had spent plenty of her life standing on the gray linoleum floor inside the kitchen of Roseberry, doing the exact same things. Sometimes it felt to China that she was just born to be in a kitchen and that there was no way around it.

Earnestine used to take her baby girl with her to the kitchen at Roseberry. She used to sit her in a cardboard box, nestled among clean rags and her old coat. She used to give her a ring of measuring spoons to play with until Emma Redd saw them in the baby's mouth and had them thrown away.

Earnestine used to take her baby girl out into the backyard to sit on an old quilt in the sun and sometimes, if Joe wasn't around, she would pull the earrings out from under the house and dangle them from her fingers against her ears. Earnestine would wonder out loud to China if she would ever have anything so pretty to call her own. Earnestine would say to her baby girl, "You'll get the pretty things, China. You wait and see."

China Redd can remember the way that teardrop of seashell looked against her mother's long, cocoa-brown neck. China can remember the sound of her mother's voice. She can remember the shape of her lips as she said, "Pretty." She can remember the way the sunlight glinted off the gold casing of the seashell earrings. China can remember the squeak of the door behind her and the shadow of her father looming over them and his hand coming down and slapping Earnestine and then snatching the earrings up off the ground where they had fallen.

China was three years old then and that night her mother curled into bed beside her and slept and the next morning her father knocked lightly on the door. He came in with tears in his eyes. He wrapped his big arms around both of them and cried. He blubbered into Earnestine's neck, "I'm sorry, Baby. But you see, Honey, no good comes from having those earrings out."

It was the first time that China could remember hearing the story of the earrings and her father told her how he had scrambled to hide them on the day that she was born, how he had scrambled to hide them to make sure that she was born right.

Joe told his baby girl that it was only by the grace of God and the earrings that their children were born healthy and strong. He cupped China's small face into the palm of his huge hand and he ran his fingers across Earnestine's cheeks and said, "I'm sorry, Sweetheart. Forgive me."

Eleven years later China followed her mother across the road to Roseberry. She began her life of dusting and cooking and cleaning for the white Redds. She began her life of standing in Roseberry's kitchen more than her own.

There came a day when all the white folks were gone from the house and Earnestine and China were enjoying the peace and quiet, carrying feather dusters from room to room and swishing them across lampshades and mantles. They carried the feather dusters up the staircase and began swiping at the frames of the white Redds' portraits that lined the staircase wall.

Earnestine patted the feathers of her duster against the canvas of each one of them and said their names to China. When she got to the one of a young boy leaning against a pink fainting couch, Earnestine patted it and said, "That's William Lars Redd. He's the boy that stole the earrings. He's the boy that drowned in the Haw River."

China leaned forward and peered at the canvas.

Her mother patted the next one and said, "That's Jennis. He was blood father to the boy that got sold. He was blood father to this boy too."

Her mother patted the next one and said, "Lula Anne Redd. She's the one had Cleavis sold. There's the earrings right there. You can see she was wearing them."

Earnestine patted the feathers of her duster against the canvas. Earnestine patted the feathers of her duster against the face of Lula Anne Redd.

5

China knew that there were other stories, stories that belonged to the white Redds, stories that she had grown up with the same as she had grown up with her own. The stories that the white Redds told could be felt by China through the things she cleaned every day.

She easily learned, standing side by side with her momma in the kitchen of Roseberry, which set of good china had been Emma's and which had belonged to Laura. China learned, standing side by side with her momma in the attic of Roseberry, which wedding dress had belonged to Lula Anne and which christening gown William Lars Redd had worn. Standing next to her momma in the parlor of Roseberry, she learned which table Mamie Redd had rested her hands on as she posed for her portrait and in the dining room she learned which tea set had belonged to Beth and which to Lula Anne.

From her momma China learned that the dips of wood in the attic stair treads were caused by the feet of house slaves, that they had slept up there and that they had rushed downstairs to close the shutters on the night of Tom's bone-chilling sigh and that it must have been a house slave that stole the earrings for Cally. Other stories were passed down from the white women they worked for.

They were passed down in phrases like, "Earnestine, do be careful with John's riding crop," or, "Do be careful with Jennis Redd's pistol. He carried it in the war, you know," or, "Do be careful with Miss Mamie's crystal."

China's mother and father laughed about it inside the walls of their little house. Earnestine said that working inside of Roseberry was like working inside a museum.

"You can't even kill a roach without hearing about who his ancestors were," Earnestine said.

China's father laughed and China learned to laugh with them. China learned to crack jokes on the white Redds just as well as her parents. China learned to do an imitation of Emma Redd that would put her momma in stitches. China learned that it was the laughter and the earrings and the grace of God that held her family together.

But there were some things that China didn't have to learn, things she seemed to have been born knowing. China just grew up knowing not to laugh in front of the white Redds, knowing to say "yes, ma'am" and "no, ma'am" and "yes, sir" and "no, sir." She just grew up knowing to agree with them most of the time, but if they said something too ridiculous to agree with, China knew to just say nothing. Pour some tea or coffee. Busy yourself with the food or the cleaning. China was born knowing when to look at them and when not to look at them. China grew up knowing how to feel the situation out.

The one story that the white Redds had that drove China's mother crazy was the story of a vine called Mamie's wisteria. China had heard the story of Mamie's wisteria nearly as much as the story of the earrings. She had heard it laughingly told around the same kerosene lanterns, beside the same washtubs, between the same rows of plants in their garden. China had seen, all her life, either her own father or Lewis or George keeping Mamie's wisteria trimmed back from the house. China had tried to remember Mamie Redd's wedding but she was only one year old at the time.

But she had touched the dress that Mamie wore. She had run her hand along its silky white material. She had fingered its lace and buttons and thought about the wisteria vine planted when she was just one year old.

Mamie's wedding dress hung in the attic of Roseberry at the end nearest the vent. There was a row of wedding dresses hanging there, one for every woman that had ever been a white Redd or married a white Redd. There were six in all. Mamie's was easy to find. It was labeled with a strip of paper pinned to the bodice.

"Mamie Redd to Joseph Parker," the paper read. "May 24, 1913."

All the wedding dresses were labeled this way. China had touched every single one. She had even touched the dress that belonged to Rose Redd, the woman whom the house was named for and whom the house had been a wedding gift to from her father and who had brought to her husband an inheritance of land and slaves.

China had touched that dress and more. She had touched Lula Anne's dress and Beth's and Laura's and in secret China had tried on Emma Redd's veil. She had stood at one end of the attic, looking out through the lacy veil and the slats of the vent towards her own little house across the dirt road. She had looked through lace and slats of wood and she had said, "I do," to an imaginary man.

China tried to imagine Mamie's wedding. She had heard that it was fancy, a fine, fancy wedding for a bride as old as Mamie Redd was. A fine, fancy wedding for a woman whose people were sure that she would never marry.

Jennis Redd was seventy-eight years old the year his daughter, Mamie, married, and he liked to say that he had survived a lot. He had survived the war, he said, and the loss of his property and the deaths of two wives and even through all that he had managed to hold on to Roseberry and most of its land.

China knew what Jennis Redd had meant when he said property. China knew that he had meant Cally and Tom and Tuly and Jed—and even Abe, who wasn't born until freedom. Even China herself, if life had gone on the way that Jennis Redd wanted it to. China Redd knew what Jennis Redd meant when he said property.

He did not mean land or cattle or even the small plot

of rocks that he had sold to Joe and Alfie. When Jennis Redd said that he had managed to hold onto Roseberry and most of its land, he meant the house and the fields that the slaves had cleared and the cemetery where the white Redds were buried and the small clearing of rocks where Cally and Tom and Tuly were laid to rest.

Jennis Redd had kept most everything intact, including his health and a room upstairs that was still papered in Confederate money—money pasted there after the war by himself and Lula Anne to keep the cold out.

But in 1913, with the little extra he had gotten from selling the land to Joe and Alfie and renting some fields to a farmer, Jennis Redd was back on his feet again and as far as anyone could tell, Roseberry was prospering.

The year that Mamie got married, Jennis Redd hired Joe's wife, Earnestine, to come help out around the house and he had wallpaper put over the old Confederate bills in the one upstairs bedroom and when his thirty-nine-year-old daughter, Mamie, announced her engagement to a man five years her junior, Jennis Redd didn't bat an eye and he went all-out for Mamie's wedding. These were the things that China heard.

He was spry enough still, China heard, to walk the bride down between the rows of chairs set out on the lawn of Roseberry. Spry enough to tie magnolia blossoms and ribbons onto the newel posts and railing of Roseberry's front porch and spry enough to vigorously shake the hand of the groom and get a lesson in driving his new Model T down the dirt road in front of the house. Jennis Redd was spry enough to dance three waltzes with his only daughter.

And the day after the wedding, Jennis Redd was spry enough still to put his foot on the blade of a shovel and dig up that damn wisteria vine that Mamie had planted before her departure.

"You planted it too close to the house," Jennis had told her.

"It will be pretty," Mamie replied. "You wait and see. Besides, I wanted to leave something here at Roseberry from me. I'm going to miss living here," Mamie said, running her hands across the back of the wicker porch swing and taking a glass of lemonade from the tray that Earnestine was offering.

"You left something, alright," Jennis said. "Wisteria. It grows like a weed, you know."

Earnestine went home that night with the baby on her hip and told Joe that Mamie Redd had planted wisteria right up next to the house. "Just outside the dining room window," Earnestine said.

"Wisteria?" Joe exclaimed. "Lord have mercy. He's not going to leave it there, is he?"

"Through the wedding," Earnestine answered. "I suspect he'll leave it there through the wedding."

It was the day after the wedding that the telegram arrived and Jennis Redd was standing out in the yard with his foot poised on the blade of the shovel. James's wife, Laura, had just told him he ought not to be exerting himself.

"Get Joe to dig it up," she hollered from the shade of the porch. "You're too old to be out in the hot sun with a shovel. It's embarrassing."

Jennis had waved his arm at her, sent her off shaking

her head, had just muttered under his breath for her to mind her own business when the telegraph arrived and after that, after getting the news that Mamie and her new husband were both killed when the Model T turned over, Jennis Redd didn't have the heart to dig up that damn vine anymore.

"Keep it pruned," he said to Joe the next day. "Just keep it pruned. You let one trail of that vine climb up on this house and I'll have your hide."

So it was Joe who first kept the wisteria vine trimmed away from the house, and after Joe got a job in town, it was Lewis and after him it was George. It was always a black man in the heat of the summer snipping on that wisteria vine and doing such a good job of keeping it trimmed back that, over the years, the white Redds came to believe it was a vine that never grew and never died and they passed the lore along like it was true. They passed the lore along from one to the next to the next until finally, Lydia Redd published it in her book, one whole chapter titled, "Mamie's Wisteria," complete with wedding pictures.

In the picture of Mamie's wedding there's a woman in the background, standing beneath a tree with a tray of drinks in her hands. It's a picture of China's mother, Earnestine, and looking at the picture, China wondered where she herself had been that day. Was she inside, trapped in a cardboard box, or was her father keeping her that day or was it the woman down the road?

China could not remember the day of Mamie Redd's wedding, but she could remember Riley's. She was thirty-five years old when Riley Redd married Lydia Carnes. China could easily remember Riley's wedding and the bitter toast he made to his new wife.

"To the rest of my life," he had said, holding his glass in the air towards Lydia. "To the rest of my life, now over, completely over."

China could remember the way that Riley had gone outside to hold his glass in the air to every departing guest. She could remember the way he had swayed back and forth, standing on the porch beneath the light of twenty white paper lanterns. China could remember the way he had taken off his shoes, his ugly bare feet and the damp footprints he had left across the floor.

China could remember the feel of the hundred-dollar bill Riley had handed her at the end of the night. China rubbed it between her fingers as she walked home, feeling her way in the dark towards the darkness of her house.

China could remember striking a match on the wall and setting it to the wick of the kerosene lamp. She could remember carrying the lamp down the hallway and easing the door to her son's bedroom open, holding the lamp high so that she could gaze at his sleeping ten-year-old face.

It's a start, China thought, thinking of the money in her pocket.

She had saved three hundred dollars already, a collection of bills and change that she kept tucked into the toe of her father's old shoe inside her closet. Now there was a hundred dollars more, given to her by a drunken Riley Redd.

It's a start.

6

China's son was the second baby born in the house that Joe and Alfie built and he wasn't born on the kitchen floor as she had been. He was born in an old wrought-iron bed that had a bent frame and sat in the room at the back, the one China's parents had shared before they both died in the same year.

It was Joe that got sick and died first, his last breath wheezed out of him in the same iron bed where China's son breathed his first.

Once her father was gone, China's mother was too lonely to stay in this world. That's how China thought of it. That's how she saw it when her mother reached over and held Joe's hand while China ran a cool washcloth across his forehead. China heard her father wheeze that last breath and she heard her mother say, "Take me with you, Joe. Take me with you," and China thought to herself, she's not long for this world, my momma. She'll be going now, soon.

Earnestine died just three months later, died in the same iron bed, died quiet. Her last breath was as quiet as a feather duster patted against the canvas of a picture.

It was after her mother died that the loneliness moved into the house with China and started living inside her heart. It woke her in the mornings and it tucked her in at nights. It walked down the lane towards Roseberry with her. It softly held her hand as she slipped the key into the lock. It was loneliness that China's son, Earnest, was born of.

He was born with the same long, skinny fingers and golden-brown skin that his father had, skin the color of pine straw, skin that China could only hope she might get to touch again, skin that belonged to a transient farm worker named Amzie Washington.

Amzie Washington showed up at Roseberry one day, standing on the back stoop with a dirty felt hat in his hands and knocking lightly on the door.

By then China had spent two years of her life waking up alone in that big iron bed and ten years of her life cutting the crusts off of store-bought bread for tiny, cookie-cutter sandwiches served at Roseberry's parties.

The only people that China saw that didn't need to be called "ma'am" or "sir" were Lewis the gardener and his son, George. Lewis was old and bent and George was young and full of wildness. China was looking for something besides old and something besides wild. China was looking for something other than loneliness to touch her inside, and by the time Amzie Washington arrived she was ripe with the need of it.

Amzie Washington stayed on at Roseberry for three weeks. He worked in the barns and the fields. He took his hat off for white people and did whatever was needed of him. He showed up on the back stoop of Roseberry at dinnertime every day. China would hand him a pie tin of food and a jar of iced tea and he would say, "Thank you," and nothing more. Amzie Washington's mouth didn't say much but his look said plenty and one day that look made China reach through the air between them and pluck a piece of straw from his hair.

He made a hard pallet out in one of the old slave cabins. He picked the middle one on the right, the very one that China was conceived in, the very one that Cally had sat outside of on a moonless Carolina night and waited for the earrings. Amzie Washington didn't know that.

He set his feet onto that split-log step every night for three weeks and he built a fire in the fireplace and stretched his legs out and rolled a cigarette. When China left Roseberry for the night, she could smell the smoke coming out of the chimney of Cally's old cabin. She could see a soft glow through the slats of the shuttered window.

Leaving Roseberry one night, China gazed down across the yard towards that soft glow. She gazed across the road at her own house, at its dark form huddled against the sky and, standing there looking, China could almost feel the coldness of the sheets on her bed. She could almost feel the hole in one of them, the hole that her toe worked through and caught in every single night. She could almost smell the smoke of her kerosene lamps and see the circle of soot on the ceiling above each one of them.

China opened the paper bag of biscuits she was taking home and counted. There were six in all. She rolled the bag tight and looked towards the cabin.

When she knocked on his door he said, "Come in," but China stood there on the split-log step. "Come in," he said again.

China wasn't planning on going in. She just wanted to

be friendly. She just wanted to drop off a bag of biscuits. They were extra, left over from dinner.

"Come in," he said again and China pushed the door open and stepped inside.

Amzie Washington was sitting on the floor by the fire. He didn't seem surprised that she was there. "Your feet must be tired," he said, patting the ground beside him. "Come on in. I won't bite."

"I brought you some biscuits," China told him.

Amzie smiled. He got up and took the bag from her, said thank you and led her to the fire.

"Your feet must be tired," he said again. "Come on now. I won't bite."

He gave China a gentle push and she sat down. Amzie Washington sat down and reached over and picked up one of her feet and lay it in his lap. He smiled at her and unlaced her shoe. He pulled her sock off slower than a sock was ever meant to be pulled off. He rubbed his fingers and his thumbs into places where she had never been touched before.

China's baby did not slide out of her as easily as Amzie Washington had slid in, nor as easily as he slid out of town the very next day, not even showing up for dinner.

On the day that he was born, Earnest seemed to be holding on to the insides of China and China's insides seemed to be holding on to him.

The midwife said, "Y'all got to let go of each other now."

But they didn't. They hung on for two hours and when Earnest finally did make it into the world, China was too weak to even pick him up. The midwife cut the umbilical cord with a kitchen knife. She washed him off and lay him on China's chest and he *crawled* his way to her breast.

China whispered, "I'd have kept him in there forever if I could have."

The midwife leaned forward and China repeated in her weak, raspy voice, "I'd have kept him in there forever."

The midwife sponged at China's face and said, "Babies were meant to be born, Honey. What's his name?"

China felt the baby's mouth tugging at her nipple and she whispered, "Earnest, after my momma."

China rested for two days before she wobbled out of bed and wrapped Earnest in a piece of a quilt and carried him outside and down the road in the early morning. Her legs shook the same as Maude's legs had shook after childbirth, on the day that she hid the earrings back where they belonged. China's legs shook like the thin branches of a tree in the wind. She felt them somewhere down below her. Her hands shook too, reaching for the key. She could see it playing against the lock before it found its way in. The eggs that China cracked that morning didn't always make it into the frying pan.

When Earnest was young China lay him in a padded cardboard box, close to the stove in the kitchen of Roseberry. When he started crawling she built a barricade of chairs and an overturned card table. She brought a ring of measuring spoons from the drawers inside her own kitchen for the baby to play with.

Every day China counted his fingers and his toes. Every day she thanked the Lord that there was such a beautiful child in this world and that he was hers. Every day, before leaving for Roseberry, China carried a kerosene lamp out into her backyard and checked to see that the earrings were safe.

After Earnest was born, China started leaving things in the snuffbox with the earrings. China left buttons and the petals of wildflowers, dropping them like offerings on top of the cloth torn from Cally's head rag. She left the fine downy feathers she'd found caught on a thorn bush. She left the first leaves of spring and the colored leaves of fall. She left the smooth brown seeds of the pawpaw fruit.

On Sundays, China took Earnest outside and let him crawl to his heart's content. She sat on the back step and watched him crawl across the rough, patched ground, watched him pick up pine cones and lob them at the cat, watched him, more times than not, find his way to the edge of the house and use the rocks of the corner piling to pull his way up and reach his long skinny fingers towards the place where the earrings were.

When China carried the kerosene lamp out to the corner of the house in the mornings, she carried baby Earnest in the other arm and he watched her reach under the house. He watched his momma opening the old snuffbox and poking her fingers inside, feeling for the earrings. He watched his momma take flower petals from the pocket of her dress and drop them in.

Earnest

7

China's offerings, the flowers and the feathers and the leaves, the buttons and the seeds and a cut nail pulled from one of the cabin logs, all helped Earnest to grow up with thick, sturdy bones. He grew up with muscles that were lean and taut. He grew up with a sharp mind and a loving heart and he was handsome, if only he could keep his mouth shut.

Earnest Redd grew up talking with a stutter. It started from the very beginning when he stuttered out his very first word.

"M . . . M . . . M . . . Momma."

The second word he stammered out was, "bi . . . bi . . . biscuit," and China knew after biscuit that there was going to be something wrong with her boy and she left more petals and buttons and feathers inside the snuff box and she prayed. Please don't let him be stupid, China prayed. Please don't let him be stupid.

He wasn't and China thanked God and tried to coach him in the ways of plain talking. She tried to hold his hands down until he had said one word plain. All she asked was just one word, spoken plain. But it didn't matter. Holding his hands down only made it worse.

The boys in school made fun of him. The girls laughed at him. They called him, "Er . . . Er . . . Er . . . Earnest." They wouldn't say it right even though they could.

Earnest grew up to be seventeen before any girl would talk to him and that was Julia. Julia who took the earrings right out of Chatham County, carried the snuffbox in her lap on a Greyhound bus heading for Raleigh. Earnest was sitting right next to her, each of them wearing gold bands on the ring fingers of their left hands. Julia kept on polishing hers on the hem of her dress and she would pick up Earnest's hand and polish his too and feel his fingers playing against the inside of her thighs. Julia kept both their rings shining like new.

She was sitting on the top step at the back of the hardware store when Earnest first saw her. Sitting there with her skirt hiked up, waiting to buy some nails.

Earnest had come for nails too. Nails and a small can of oil. His mother had told him that morning to fix the loose step on the front porch and while he was at it, could he try to grease the hinges on the screen door?

"It squawking something awful," China had said, as she wrote out a list on the back of an old envelope. Sixteen penny nails, a can of oil, the smallest size.

"You just go to the back door of the hardware store and knock," China told him. "Hand them this list. Don't try to tell them what you want."

The white shopkeepers in town had shown no patience for Earnest's stuttering. Once China had sent him to the back of the dime store for thread and the clerk had slammed the door in his face because Earnest was taking so long to string the words, "thread," and "blue," together. He couldn't get the two of them to come side by side inside his mouth and the more she glared at him, the harder it got, until finally she slammed the door and stalked off.

Earnest had felt the wind of the door before he heard it slam against the frame and it made him so mad that he went around the corner to the front of the store and marched right past the 'Whites Only' sign. Earnest slammed the change his mother had given him down on the counter and said, clear as a bell, "Thread. Blue."

That was the thing about Earnest. When he was mad enough he could talk as plain as anyone.

The woman sold him that thread, as surprised to see a black person standing in a whites-only dime store as she was that Earnest Redd could talk. She even put it in a brown paper bag for him and Earnest meant to say "thank you" but he could feel his tongue tying up in knots again as he realized what he'd done.

It was the same feeling when he first saw Julia sitting on the top step outside the back door of the hardware store. He could feel his tongue stiffening inside his mouth, stiffening and going loose at the same time and he nearly turned around and went home, but Julia spoke first. She said hello and Earnest nodded.

"Don't you talk?" Julia asked.

Earnest nodded again.

"What's your name?"

"Er . . . Er . . . Er . . . Earnest," he said and then he looked down at his shoes. They were dirty.

"My daddy stuttered," Julia said. "It's nothing to be ashamed of."

Earnest fell in love right then. And as if it wasn't enough that she was pretty and nice, she kept on sitting there with her dress hiked up. From where he stood, Earnest could see the bright white of her panties against the soft brown skin of her thighs, but when he saw a white man pass by and look, Earnest Redd said as quiet and plain as anyone could ever hope, "You ought to put your legs together."

Julia smiled and put her feet down on the lower step. "Where do you live?" she asked.

He pointed down the highway and managed to eke out, "Across from the old Roseberry plantation."

"Plantation days are over," Julia replied.

"Th . . . Th . . . That'd b . . . b . . . be n . . . n . . . n . . . nice," Earnest said and Julia laughed and that was the first time that Earnest Redd thought about the earrings and how much he would like to give them to her.

She told him that she was visiting her aunt, staying in Chatham County for the summer while a new man courted her momma. Or her momma courted a new man. Julia said she didn't know which way it was with her momma anymore. She said she could never figure who was courting who.

She said she used to live with her daddy but he died two years ago.

"I won't tell you how it happened," she said, and Earnest knew that he must have been killed by a white man and that it must have had something to do with the way he talked, in which case Earnest didn't want to know. He'd had his share of trouble there too.

"I paint," Julia said. "Do you do anything artistic?"

Earnest shook his head.

"What do your folks do?"

"M . . . M . . . Momma works at Ro . . . Ro . . . Roseberry. My daddy's gone."

"Gone where?"

Earnest shrugged. "Ju . . . Ju . . . Just g . . . gone."

He saw her again the next day, standing out back of the dime store and the day after that, drinking a soda down at the gas station, the one that was owned by a black man.

The next day Julia came to his house, walked the four miles from town down the highway and turned into the hard-packed lane across the road from Roseberry. It wasn't difficult to find.

Earnest was nailing down the loose step when she came walking up and when he was done they sat down beside each other and listened to the birds and Julia slipped her hand into his.

"D . . . D . . . D . . . ," Earnest started.

"We don't have to talk," Julia said. "We can kiss instead."

It was the day after his seventeenth birthday and a week later Earnest crawled under the house and felt along the corner piling for the earrings. When he found the smooth metal of the snuffbox, he pulled it out, listened to it scrape against the rocks, saw the glint of tin in the little bit of light there was. Earnest sat in the dirt with the snuff box in his lap, sat in the cool, dank air under the house, sat right next to holes in the soil that the doodle bugs made.

Earnest took the earrings and carried them down the road to Julia. She was sitting on the step of her aunt's house, sitting there with her skirt hiked up again. Earnest smiled and didn't say anything. He just sat down beside her and lay his hand on her knee and placed the snuffbox in her lap.

He watched Julia as she twisted the cap off and blew his mother's old dried flowers off the top, like dust. He watched as she plucked the old cut nail out and tossed it on the ground. When she pushed aside the shreds of cloth and cotton and held one dangling earring in the sunlight, Earnest stammered out the words he'd been planning.

"I . . . I . . . It's a sh . . . sh . . . shell called abo . . . abo . . . abolene, and it reminds me of your eyes."

Julia lay the earring in the palm of her hand and peered closely at it. She traced one finger along its gold trim. She looked at Earnest and said, "What's it called again?"

"A . . . A . . . Abolene."

Julia smiled. She took his hand in hers and corrected him. "Abalone," she said. "It's a shell called abalone."

China was making bread when he told her. He sat at the kitchen table and traced one finger along the faded red and white checks of the tablecloth.

"I . . . I . . . I . . . g . . . g . . . got something to t . . . tell . . . you," Earnest said.

"I know you do," China replied.

China knew they were gone. She had looked for them that morning, crawled under the house with a pocketful of rose petals meant as one of her offerings. China's hands had groped along the rough rocks of the corner piling, searching for the cool tin of the snuffbox, searching the rocks until her fingers bled. The petals had fallen from her pocket into a trail, back and forth along the ground below the corner piling, a line of pink rose petals zigzagging across the damp ground beneath her house.

When China realized that the earrings were gone, she sat down on the back step and cried and even now China's fingers bled. They left spots in the dough that she was kneading, snowflakes of fingerprints and swirls of blood that were the same color as the petals dropped beneath the house.

"J . . . J . . . Julia," Earnest stammered.

"You gave the earrings to her?" China asked.

China knew of Julia. She had seen them together on the steps one day. She had squinted her eyes as she stood on the back stoop of Roseberry and shook the dust out of a rug. She had squinted her eyes tight and peered at her own house and wondered what girl it was that sat so close to her son. China had asked him her name that very night and he had told her.

"Ju . . . Ju . . . Julia."

When China asked if he had given the earrings to

this girl named Julia he pressed his finger into a red check on the tablecloth and then a white one and then a red one again.

"Answer me," China said and Earnest stammered out his answer, confirming the worst for China.

She closed her eyes and imagined it, seeing the earrings on the lobes of that young girl, seeing her wearing them all over Chatham County so that anyone could ask her where they came from and Julia could say, "Earnest Redd gave them to me. The boy that lives across from Roseberry. He gave them to me."

China feared it. Feared the possibility of Lydia Redd or her husband Riley or some other white person who had visited Roseberry, seeing the earrings and recognizing them from the portrait of Lula Anne that hung on the staircase wall. China feared Lydia Redd or her husband Riley or any other white person knowing that somehow something had been stolen from them a long time ago. Something stolen back when they weren't supposed to lose anything and back when they felt that they had lost it all.

China patted the mound of bread dough like a baby and wiped one floury hand across the front of her dress, smearing it with a track of dusty white and the faint pink of bloody stripes. China was standing on the very spot where she was born when she turned around and faced her son.

"Those earrings," China began. "They've been in our family for generations," she said. "Generations. They came from Roseberry." China swept her hand towards the front of the house. "They're not meant to go courting with."

"Th . . . Th . . . They re . . . re . . . reminded me of her eyes," Earnest stammered.

China sighed. "Don't you remember?" she asked. "Abe gave those earrings to Maude for a wedding present. Don't you remember what happened?"

China turned back towards her work, sprinkling flour across the top of the dough and covering it with a clean dishcloth. When she sat down she reached across the table for her boy's hand.

"You could have any girl you wanted if you didn't stutter so," China told him.

"This . . . the . . . one . . . one . . . one . . . I . . . I . . . I . . . want," Earnest said.

"You got to get those earrings back, Son. She can't go wearing them around town. What if someone recognizes them?" Earnest screwed up his face. He squinted at her and said, "Ju . . . Ju . . . Julia . . . says . . . we . . . we . . . g . . . g . . . got the n . . . n . . . n . . . name wrong. It's a . . . a . . . a . . . abalone. Rhymes with baloney," he added.

This is how Julia had coached Earnest into remembering the new word. Abalone. Rhymes with baloney.

China repeated it. Abalone. Earnest nodded, to show her that she had got it right.

"Is this the girl you want?" China asked.

Earnest nodded again.

"Then you got to tell her the truth. You got to tell her that you stole those earrings from your own family and that if she keeps them out in the open like that, you won't ever have a healthy child. There's no telling what could happen to your babies if Julia keeps those earrings out in the open," China said. "They've got to stay in our family, Son."

Earnest poked at the tablecloth some more.

"They've got to stay in the family," China repeated.

"Th . . . Th . . . Then I . . . I'll m . . . m . . . marry her," Earnest said.

China served the bread at Earnest's wedding. It was the bread with her own rose petal fingerprints baked into it, her own grief swirling through the dough like the colors in the earrings. The guests commented on its flavor and when one of them asked for the recipe China said that it was an heirloom and could never be given away and then she cried.

Julia wanted to wear the earrings. Earnest caught her spraying them with canned oil. He caught her working the clasps back and forth and when he saw this he lay his hand on hers and said, gentle and as clear as a bell, "Don't."

"They're mine," Julia said.

"They're ours," Earnest replied and then he stuttered the same words he had stuttered to his mother on the day that she was baking wedding bread.

"I . . . I . . . I . . . g . . . g . . . got something to t . . . tell . . . you," he said.

Julia was a patient girl for being just seventeen. She sat beside him and guessed his words, fed him what she thought the next line to be was. She sat beside him and listened until she'd heard the whole story of Cally and Cleavis and the earrings. She sat beside him with her hand on his knee and listened until she knew all about

Tom's bone-chilling sigh and how it had circled Roseberry like wind, until she knew all about Maude crawling outside to hide the earrings after her first child had died, until she knew all about how China was born quick on a kitchen floor.

It took two hours for Earnest to tell it all and when he was done Julia went to China and put her arms around her and said, "They'll be safe with me."

China grabbed Julia's arm. She dug her fingers into her daughter-in-law's skin and said, "Hide them. They were never meant to see the light of day," China whispered.

"They won't," Julia promised, but it was a promise that she didn't keep.

The earrings rode in her lap on the Greyhound bus to Raleigh and after they arrived at their furnished basement apartment, Julia set them on the dresser, next to her mirror and her hand cream and the cloudy jar of watercolor brushes she used to paint with.

Julia forgot all about hiding the earrings. In their cool basement apartment in Raleigh, the story of Cally and Tom and Cleavis seemed as far away as the headwaters of the Haw River. In their cool basement apartment in Raleigh, Roseberry and Chatham County seemed like a hot, muggy dream.

Every week China called from the phone that hung on the wall in the kitchen of Roseberry. Lydia Redd kept track of these calls and deducted them from China's pay, but China didn't have a phone at home and she needed to check on her boy.

The house felt empty without him. The house felt empty

without the earrings. There was nothing at home for her to tend to anymore, except for the azaleas and the cat.

Every time China called she asked where the earrings were, always afraid to raise her voice inside of the very house they were stolen from, always afraid that if Julia or Earnest talked too loud on their phone in Raleigh they would be heard inside the kitchen of Roseberry.

Julia always answered that the earrings were safe but Earnest would stammer out, "O . . . O . . . On th . . . Th . . . The dr . . . dr . . . dresser," and China would look around the kitchen and purse her lips together and hiss, "Shhh. Shhh. Someone might hear you."

China Redd started having night sweats when Julia got pregnant. She had them every night for nine months. She woke up every morning with the sheets smelling sour and stale and every day she pulled an old cane-bottom chair up close to the phone in the kitchen of Roseberry and she whispered into the receiver, "Julia. Julia, honey. You got to hide those earrings. The baby's not safe if you don't hide those earrings."

After a while Julia started handing the phone to Earnest if he was home and hanging up if he wasn't. Eight months into the pregnancy, they stopped answering at all and China sat hovering in the corner of Roseberry's kitchen, listening to the phone in a basement apartment in Raleigh ring and ring and ring. By then she had spent more than she earned on phone calls.

Lydia Redd commented on it, asking if there was anything wrong and China answered, "No, ma'am." She reckoned she was just a nervous mother.

Lydia nodded. She knew what it was to be a nervous mother. Her own son, Coyle, was six years old that year, as wild and unpredictable as any six-year-old boy could be. Lydia Redd knew what it was to be a nervous mother.

Her husband, Riley, always told her that she worried too much. He had even told it to her on the day that they were married, when she had complained about his drinking as she watched him down one glass of bourbon after another, proposing toasts with every one, proposing toasts until the toasts became bitter.

"To the rest of my life," he had said finally. "Now over. Completely over."

The guests had started leaving then, clearing their throats and gathering their gloves and hats and saying what a wonderful event it had been.

Riley stood on the porch with his shoes off and his necktie undone and he raised his glass to every car as it drove off in a cloud of dust. When the last guest was gone it was just him and Lydia left in their wedding finery and Riley turned away from her and stumbled into the dining room where China was clearing the food and rolling up the starched white tablecloth.

"Go on home," he said. He pulled a hundred-dollar bill out of his pocket and handed it to China. "Go on home," he said. "My wife will clean it up."

China

9

In all the years that China worked inside Roseberry she saw only two babies born there, and something in the landscape was torn down both times. The first baby was Riley and his father, John, had the old kitchen house torn down. The second baby was Coyle and Riley Redd got drunk and drove the tractor into the old cabins at the edge of the woods, knocking down every one of them.

Riley was born, red-faced and squalling, the very same year that China started working with her mother. It was five months later that John Redd, Riley's father, decided to have the old kitchen house torn down.

He hired a crew of black men, bossed and paid by a white man, and China stood with her mother in the upstairs window of the nursery and watched it come down. They watched the men crawl across the cabin with hammers in their hands. They watched each board drop into a pile until the kitchen house was just an empty frame and soon it came down too. They watched the men pick up each board and toss it into the back of a truck. They watched the chimney become a pile of rocks.

Earnestine had the new baby, Riley, propped on her hip and he was holding a fistful of her hair crumpled inside one tiny white hand. China's mother kept on trying to untangle his fingers and get her head free.

When the chimney came down, Earnestine reached for her daughter's hand and held it.

"Maude cooked there," she said, shaking her head from side to side. "Maude was a good cook."

"We're still cooks," China replied.

Earnestine pointed out the window. "Right there where the truck's parked, that's where my first labor pain struck."

In four days' time, it was all gone. The ground where the kitchen house had once stood was raked clean and China thought it looked like a brown scab in the glossy green grass of the yard. Lewis and George planted rose-bushes in the brown dirt scab, six lines of them as straight and neat as the cotton fields used to be, and when Riley started crawling, John Redd had Lewis fence the whole thing in with white picket.

China felt like something that belonged to them was gone. China imagined Maude stirring the pots that simmered there or standing on the hearth and wiping the sweat out of her eyes or carrying dishes of steaming cooked food to the big house and serving it to Jennis and Lula Anne. China felt pieces of herself being taken away with every board of the kitchen house.

Looking out the window now, while she stood next to her momma washing dishes, there was nothing but nakedness and a new rose garden, laid out like the lines in the books she used to read before she'd had to quit school.

The day after the last board was hauled off was a Sunday and when it got close to dusk, China and Earnestine walked out into the field beside their house. They liked to go there on Sundays to watch the sunset and look for Joe coming home from the river with a string full of fish and a pole on his shoulder. China liked the rocks that lay at the foot of the oak tree. It was the best place of all to watch for a sunset or a father coming home from fishing.

The rocks were different sizes, big ones and small ones and one huge one rolled up against the trunk of that old tree. China could climb to the top of that one and see across the road to Roseberry. She could see the tall yellow house with the moss-green shutters. She could see the well house and the back porch and the corner of the fence surrounding the new rose garden.

"Is it because of the snake?" China asked. "Is it because of the snake that he tore down the kitchen house?"

"I reckon it is," her mother answered.

China had heard the story about John Redd and the snake, the way that he had nearly planted one bare foot on the back of a copperhead, stretched out across the smooth, worn floorboards of the kitchen house. He was just five years old then and his screams had called Joe up from the pigpen where he was building a farrowing hut. It had been Joe that grabbed the hoe that was leaning against the fence and come running across the field with it.

By the time Laura Redd had reached her son, that snake was dead, lying in two writhing pieces on the floor of the kitchen house and Joe was holding John's head against his sweat-stained shirt, laying his large brown hands across John's blond hair, saying, "It's alright now. That snake is dead."

Joe Redd was seventeen years old at the time. It was four years before he met the girl that he would marry. Five years before he and Alfie would begin building the rock foundations for their new house. Six years before he would walk with Earnestine past the kitchen house on the way to his new home.

China figured it was because of the snake that John Redd had the kitchen house torn down. She figured that John Redd didn't want anything to happen to his boy, the same way of any parent. But China couldn't figure anything but drunkenness and pure meanness for Riley Redd tearing down the cabins.

It was five weeks after Coyle's birth, and China was thirty-six years old now and she had spent twenty-two of those years working inside of Roseberry. Her momma was gone. Her daddy was gone. Her son, Earnest, was twelve years old and being held back in school, the teachers saying he was stupid and China knowing it wasn't true. Earnest just couldn't get his words to go together.

China stood at the same window she had stood at with her mother and she watched Riley Redd bump the old blue tractor across the field.

"He can't be plowing," China said. "It's too wet to plow."

Lydia Redd was standing right next to her, wearing her green cotton nightgown and holding the new baby.

"He's tearing down the cabins," Lydia said.

They watched the old blue tractor ram into the corner of the first cabin. Riley Redd backed it out before the logs tumbled. Then he rammed it again and again backed it out quickly. The roof caved in and the doorway crumpled.

"Riley's going to kill himself," Lydia said.

China held her breath and watched. He moved to the next one and then the one after that, the very one that she was conceived in and the very one that she had lain beside Amzie Washington in while firelight danced across the dark rough logs. It was Cally's cabin and in ten minutes it was gone to a tumble of logs and rocks and tin, the very tin that China's father and uncle had salvaged from a barn and pieced together on top of their own roof.

China had the same feeling that she'd had when the kitchen house was bulldozed. Something lost. Something gone at the whim of its owner. Never mind the lives that were lived there. Never mind the honeysuckle growing wild along the walls of the kitchen house and the way she liked its smell better than the cloying smell of the roses. Never mind the way the cabins had all leaned in the same direction, like wind-swept trees on a hilltop with their roots digging into rocks and holding on for dear life. Never mind the haunting way that a chimney would fall down on its own. Never mind the mounds of moss-covered rocks. Never mind the flash of blue as a skink slithered between them.

There was nothing beautiful about this, China thought, as Riley Redd pulled the tractor back and then forward again, ramming the next cabin.

It was then that the new baby, Coyle, squawked in Lydia's arms. He gurgled and squirmed and Lydia handed him to China and said, "He needs his bottle."

"Yes, ma'am," China said.

"I'll be in bed," Lydia said. She took one more look out the window and then walked out of the room, her pink slippers softly patting at the floor.

Earnest

10

Earnest was twelve years old when Coyle Redd was born. He would stir the pots and check the biscuits while his mother tended Coyle. He would watch her wrap her strong brown arms around the little white baby, all pink-faced and rolled up warm in a soft yellow blanket. Earnest would watch his mother sit in the rocking chair pulled into Roseberry's kitchen, feeding the baby his bottle. Earnest would watch his mother lay the baby up on her shoulder and pat his back until she heard his small belch of gas.

Earnest didn't like going to Roseberry after school, but it was where his momma was and he was always glad to see his momma after a day at school. Earnest didn't like Riley Redd and he was always glad when he didn't see Mr. Redd's car parked in the driveway. Riley Redd made fun of him. Riley Redd called him Er . . . Er . . . Er . . . Earnest, just like the boys at school did.

His momma told him she didn't know what made Riley Redd so mean, but she said that he was mean from the get-go. She said that Riley used to tug at her own momma's hair and then hers if she ever let him get hold of it. She said that Riley used to drop bugs into glasses of water just to watch them suffer and drown. She said that Riley used to pull the cat's tail until the cat finally moved across the road and took up with Joe and Earnestine and China.

"That's how we got that old cat," his mother told him. "She just followed us home one day and never went back."

China would shake her head at Earnest whenever Riley left the room. China would look at Earnest and quietly mouth the words, "Mean. Mean from the get-go."

Earnest was twelve years old the year that Coyle Redd was born and sixteen the first time he ever saw Riley Redd turn on his own child with a belt in his hand.

It was on a Christmas night and China and Earnest were both drawn outside by the deep yelling of Riley's voice and the slamming of doors and the snap of leather in the air. They stood in the dark of their porch and watched Riley Redd drag his son down the steps and across the yard to the scruff of grass beneath the pole lamp. Earnest was sixteen years old and taller than China now and he couldn't bury his face in the folds of her dress the way he wanted to. He just stood there and watched as Lydia Redd's hands fluttered against her husband's arms, trying to get him to stop. Earnest just stood there and watched until Riley Redd stopped long enough to push her down. He saw Coyle crumpled on the ground, his arms and hands covering his head, his stomach facing down, letting his back take the brunt of the blows.

Earnest just stood there and watched until he heard a deep bellowing that he thought might be coming from him. He felt a shaking that he thought might be an earthquake. He heard a splitting howl that he was sure must be their house tearing apart into two pieces.

Suddenly Earnest felt his mother's hands covering his eyes and ears and pushing him inside. He heard himself trying to say her name, the name that he knew her by. "M . . . M . . . M . . . Momma." He tried and tried but it wouldn't come out and he felt her pushing him onto the couch and then the warmth of his mother's shoulder.

China rocked him. "Shhh," she said. "Shhhh. That's over there, not over here. Shhhh. That's over there."

Over here, in the house that Joe and Alfie had built, there was one strand of colored Christmas lights strung across the mantel. There were three open gifts lying on the floor in front of the heater. One was a sweater and another a pair of shoes. They belonged to Earnest and had come from his momma. The other was an apron. It was all that he could think of to give her.

Over here, in the house that Joe and Alfie had built, there was the hiss of the gas heater and Earnest could feel its heat glowing into his toes and skin. Over here Earnest could feel that what he had thought was an earthquake was the shaking of his own body. What he had thought was their house tearing in two had been something inside of him, cracking apart like a piece of split wood, the wind of grain holding onto itself, but coming apart all the same. Over here Earnest struggled to get up but China held him down and kept on rocking him.

"Why?" Earnest asked, as plain as day. "Why?" He still had his head muffled down into the crook of China's arm.

China shook her head. "I don't know," she said. "I've seen it before. I was hoping you never would."

In the mornings after Coyle got a beating from his

daddy, China would see the bruises and welts peeking out of the collar of his long-sleeved shirt. She would bake him cookies and hold his hand and when Lydia Redd came into the kitchen to lightly lay a kiss on her son's forehead, China would get up from the table and busy herself at the sink. She would look out into the yard at the rose garden and think about the kitchen house. She would look out into the yard at the rose garden and listen for the swish of the swinging door that meant Lydia Redd had left.

"Can't w . . . w . . . we . . . ," Earnest started.

"Do something?" China finished for him. "What are we going to do? Report it? Have a talk with him?" China shook her head. "I can't do anything."

"Sw . . . Sw . . . Sw . . . Sweep," Earnest said. "T . . . T . . . T . . . Turn on the po . . . po . . . porch light a . . . a . . . a . . . and sweep. Go do it now."

That's how China Redd came to sweep her porch on Christmas night in 1952. That's how China Redd came to sweep her porch every time she heard a scuffle starting up across the street.

That's what China Redd learned she could do and she learned it from her boy, Earnest. China learned to turn on her porch light, keep a high-wattage bulb in there, start singing a hymn as loud as she could, start yelling the hymn if she had to, all the while scraping the furniture across the floor as she poked the broom in the corners and knocked the cobwebs down and swept the bejesus out of the buckled floorboards of her porch.

China swept and sang as Riley railed out of control in the yard across the highway. China swept and sang and kept sweeping and kept singing, but never looked up. Never acknowledged that there was anyone who might be watching. Just swept and sang and swept and sang until eventually Riley Redd noticed it and stopped beating Coyle out of sheer embarrassment.

Coyle Redd came to depend on it. He came to pray to China's house, pray to the light on the porch to come on bright, pray to the broom to sweep hard and long and furious, pray to China to sing with all her might.

Coyle Redd came to depend on it, but he never knew it was Earnest's idea. Coyle hardly knew Earnest at all because Earnest left for Raleigh the following year.

Earnest and Julia took earrings that Coyle never knew existed. Earnest and Julia took a piece of China away from Chatham County, away from the house that Joe and Alfie had built, away even from what was known as Roseberry. Earnest and Julia took the earrings away from Chatham County and neither of them ever brought them back.

China

11

On the day that her granddaughter was born, China's night sweats stopped and she woke up that morning as comfortable and dry as talcum powder. When she stood in the mirror and combed her hair, her eyes fell on the reflection of the clean sheets stacked in the chair behind her. Until then, she had not thought of it, had not thought of the dry bed she had just risen from, or the sweet smell of sleep as opposed to the sourness of sweat.

The sheets on the chair behind her were fresh off the clothesline and smelling like summer. There were three sets folded there, three different patterns creating a rotation of linen that China had maintained all throughout Julia's pregnancy. A rotation of linen that had let China slide into a clean bed every night, just as surely as she woke up in a drenched one.

Seeing those sheets stacked in the chair like that made China stop and lay the comb down on the dresser. She ran her hands along her arms and felt the dryness of her skin. She went to the bed and lowered her head and breathed deeply the smell of clean linen just slept on.

"My grandbaby's born today," China said to the house she was born in. "My grandbaby's born today."

Sure enough, there was a note for her on the kitchen counter of Roseberry. It said, "Earnest called. A baby girl. Five pounds, six ounces. Mother and baby are fine."

"I didn't catch the baby's name," Lydia wrote. "Abby something."

China called.

"Abolene," Julia said. "We named her Abolene. After the earrings."

China lowered her voice and cut her eyes towards the door to the dining room. Behind it she could hear Riley turning the pages of the paper. She could hear Lydia primly setting her coffee cup down in its saucer. China cut her eyes to the table in the kitchen where Coyle sat, happily crunching down on a piece of toast. China lowered her voice and asked, "Where are they?"

"They're safe," Julia said. "And so is my baby."

China took two days off work to catch a Greyhound bus to Raleigh. Two days off work to see this baby who had been named after earrings, to make sure for herself that this new child had all her fingers and toes and a healthy cry.

Sitting on the seat of the bus and watching the land slide by, watching the fields and the houses and the children playing in the yards slip away behind her, China whispered the name of the new baby to herself. She whispered it over and over and over again.

"Abolene. Abolene. Abolene."

China thought to herself of Cleavis sold away, no one knowing where to and all because of this word *abolene* and now there's a baby with this name. A baby named

Abolene, after earrings not hidden. A baby named Abolene, after a mistake a little white boy made in 1861. A baby named Abolene, not abalone, not the word that rhymes with baloney, not that word.

The baby Abolene was like a little raisin rolled up in a soft pink blanket and she looked just like China's son. She had the same soft brown skin and big brown eyes. She gave the same look to Julia as she suckled her breast that Earnest had given to China not so many years ago.

"I reckon she didn't take anything from me," Julia said.

"Life," China replied.

She leaned over and touched the baby's soft face. Held her hands and examined each little moon of fingernail. Held her toes and watched them curl.

Earnest stood behind his mother watching and China asked, "How you feeling, Son?"

"I feel good," Earnest said. His words were as smooth and dependable as the air. "I feel good." He draped one arm around his mother's shoulders. After Abolene was born, China never heard her son stutter again.

China called them every week, always on Fridays, always from the yellow wall phone hanging in Roseberry's kitchen.

Coyle was six years old that year and still taking his breakfast at the white enamel-topped table that sat in the middle of the floor. China fed him toast and milk. He never wanted anything else.

She served Riley and Lydia in the dining room, coffee and eggs and bacon and toast. She whisked empty dishes away and washed them and dusted and polished and all the time China thought about this new baby named

Abolene. China worried about it. A healthy girl, but would she stay that way?

China called them every week and at the end of each call she would say only one thing. "I think you ought to hide those earrings."

Earnest would answer that they would. Julia would say it too. But they didn't.

China knew. She knew it by the way she woke up every night at 2 A.M. She knew it by the way her eyes flew open out of the dead of sleep. She knew it by the first waking thought she had. Is the baby alright?

She asked Mrs. Redd if there were any old things that she could have to send to Earnest and Julia, and Lydia came into the kitchen one day with a box of Coyle's old baby clothes. She set it on the white enamel table.

"These are mostly boy's things," Lydia said. "But for a baby, I don't guess it matters."

"No, ma'am," China said. And, "Thank you."

"What is that name again?" Lydia asked.

"Abolene," China answered.

"Do you know where it came from?" Lydia asked.

"It's been in our family for years," China said.

"I've never heard it before," Lydia said.

"It's distant," China replied.

Lydia nodded. She glanced out the window at Riley packing camping gear to take on a hunting trip.

"He's taking Coyle to the river shack," Lydia said. "So I guess it's going to be just us girls for a few days."

"Yes, ma'am."

"We'll get a lot done," Lydia said, shoving the box of

baby clothes across the kitchen table.

"Yes, ma'am."

China dreaded being alone in the house with Lydia. She dreaded the inspections behind every door. The peering into the corners of the cabinets. The wash that Lydia would send back to be done and done again. Nothing suited her when Riley was gone with Coyle. China guessed that Lydia was worried. China guessed that anything might be better than being married to Riley Redd and watching him take your son into the woods with a backpack full of booze and a gun slung over his shoulder. China guessed that anything might be better than that. Most anything, anyway.

Lydia looked again out the window at her husband. "We'll get a lot done," she repeated, and patted the top of the box.

China stood there and listened to the swinging door that led from the kitchen squeak on its hinges. She listened to Lydia's footsteps crossing hardwood floors and padding across the rugs. She listened to the springs in the couch creak as Lydia Redd sat down and picked up her embroidery.

China opened the box and pulled out a tiny, blue seersucker suit. She remembered it. She remembered each little cotton outfit as she held them up one by one. She remembered scrubbing the stains out of them and washing them and hanging them outside on the line. China remembered folding them and putting them away and then later, taking them out of the drawers and jamming Coyle's fat little baby legs into them.

China wished that Earnest and Julia and the new baby, Abolene, lived closer. She wished that she could hold Abolene's feet and coax them into the legs of the seersucker pants. She wished that the earrings were back where they belonged.

China closed the box with masking tape and in large black letters she wrote, "Miss Abolene Redd, 506 Tinkerton Street, Raleigh, North Carolina." China walked along the highway to town the next afternoon to post the box of clothes to Raleigh.

It was a year later that Earnest disappeared. China got the phone call on a Thursday morning. Lydia Redd pushed the swinging door to the kitchen open and told her that her daughter-in-law was on the line. China's heart started beating too fast in her chest. She wiped her soapy hands on her apron and picked up the yellow receiver and the first thing she said was, "Julia? The baby?"

"Is Earnest there?" Julia asked.

China could hear Abolene crying in the background and she sighed out loud to feel the safety of her.

"Did he say he was coming here?"

"No, ma'am," Julia said. "He never said anything. He left for work on Monday and never showed up again." Julia started crying. "We had a fight," she said. "He was chopping the onions wrong."

There was a catch in China's heart. It was a catch as strong and stubborn as a stuck door. It was a catch just like she felt when she searched for the earrings along the rocks of the corner piling and only found the blood in her fingers.

"Not since *Monday?*" China exclaimed. Her words rang

against the kitchen walls, like the echo of a gunshot.

China left the next day. She took the bus again and rode in the back seat of a cab for the first time in her life. It cost five dollars and twenty-three cents to get from the bus station in Raleigh to 506 Tinkerton Street, and China counted the change out carefully. She gave the man no more and no less.

Julia was sitting in bed with the baby. There were clothes littering the floor and a bucket of diapers unwashed and the windows closed up as tight as a tick.

China stayed a week. She picked up clothes and walked baskets full of clothes to the laundromat a mile away. She folded them and placed them on hangers and put them away in closets and dressers. Her own son's pants and shirts. His socks and underwear. She washed and folded these things and put them away, the same as she did Julia's skirts and dresses and the tiny suits that now belonged to Abolene.

The earrings were there, still cupped inside cotton and cloth inside the snuffbox, but not sitting on Julia's dresser shoved behind the pot of face powder and the tubes of watercolor that she painted with. Instead, the snuffbox of earrings was always in Julia's hands. If she was sleeping, the snuffbox was shoved under her pillow with her hands clasped around it. If she was watching TV, she held it in her lap. If she was thinking about Earnest, Julia would twist the cap off and hold one earring in the air in front of her.

"You've got to pull yourself together," China said. "You've got a baby to care for."

"He'll be back," Julia insisted.

"Of course he will," China replied, but by the end of the week, after the house was clean and put together and Julia was out of bed and taking care of the baby and there had still been no word from Earnest, China said, "You better get yourself a job." She changed Abolene's diaper for the last time. She cleaned her and powdered her and took the diaper pins out of her mouth.

China said, "Lots of women raised babies by themselves." China said, "Why don't you let me take those earrings back home with me?" China said, "It might help to put them back where they belong."

"They belong to Abolene now," Julia answered. "They're not yours anymore."

Three months after Earnest disappeared, China had a phone installed in her house. It was a heavy black phone and it sat on a thin, half-round table at the end of the hallway, just outside the bathroom door.

China had it installed after the police in Raleigh called Roseberry and left the message for her to call back. It was after they told her that Earnest was dead, gave her this news with Lydia Redd standing right there in the kitchen with her, gave her this news while China was cleaning Coyle Redd's hands with a warm, wet cloth.

They'd found a body, they said. They'd found a body with its hands tied behind its back, lying in a wooded area not far from 506 Tinkerton Street. They'd found a body shot three times through the chest. It was similar to the descriptions of Earnest. A black man, same build. It must have involved contraband, the police said. It must have been a deal gone wrong.

They took Earnest's name off the missing persons' list and mailed an envelope of the few things that were in the body's pants pockets. They mailed the envelope to Julia and Julia opened it and poured the contents on her bed. It was a watch that she didn't recognize. A key that did not fit her house. A wedding band that could have been his. A handful of change that did not amount to much. Julia mailed the envelope to China. "These don't look like his things," she wrote.

China refused to believe that they were and she got a phone of her own and for six months she called the precinct in Raleigh and talked to the D.A.

"My boy's not dead," she said.

"We know it's hard," the man told her.

China knew in her heart it wasn't her son and she never claimed the body. Neither did Julia. There was never a funeral or a service or a tombstone with Earnest Redd's name on it. The only prayer uttered for the man found in the woods was by China and it was, "Please don't let it be Earnest."

Over time China stopped calling the D.A. in Raleigh and she took the watch and the key and the ring and the handful of change and she dropped them into the crevice of the corner piling where the earrings used to be. She listened to these things fall and clink into the cracks between the rocks. They were never her boy's things and they were never retrievable.

Phone bills and letters from Julia filled China's rusty mailbox now. Julia wrote regularly with news of the jobs she'd found and the struggle to send herself to beauty college and at last her graduation. Julia filled the letters with news of Abolene and pictures she had drawn on scrap paper, swirls of color that were just like the shells in the earrings. Julia sent pictures of Abolene growing strong and tall and sinewy, just like Earnest had.

China walked to Roseberry in the dawn and home in the dusk. She sat on the porch in the dark and gazed across the street towards the lights of the house she worked in. She watched Lydia and Riley and sometimes Coyle drift like shadows across the windows and if there was the sound of argument or leather snapping in the air, China would turn on her porch light and slam her own door and sweep her own porch in furious clouds of dust.

After all this time, didn't they know? A child could be taken away from you. Even now, a child could be taken away and he would be gone, like coins dropped down a well and sinking to the bottom. His presence would be the never-ending ripple on your heart.

Coyle

12

Coyle Redd was thirteen years old when he finally wrested that belt from his father's hands. He was thirteen years old and there had been many mornings that he had twisted his body around to look at the bruises on his back. There had been many mornings that he had seen his own father's initials there, bruised into his back by the brass metal of his belt buckle. 'R.R.' Bruised there just as if he had been branded.

There had been many mornings that Coyle Redd had felt China's hand across his forehead, had felt her sink down across the table from him, had felt her get up and busy herself with the dishes whenever his mother came into the room. There had been plenty of mornings that Coyle had put on one of the brand-new shirts that were kept in his closet and wondered what had become of the old one, the one he had been wearing the night before, the one that was probably ripped and crusted with blood.

On a summer night during Coyle's thirteenth year there had been another evening of tensed silence after dinner, the only sounds being the glugs of Riley's bourbon pouring across ice cubes, the pages of a book turning and the thread of Lydia Redd's embroidery going through cloth.

Coyle was the one who had been reading, and when he

went into his father's den to shelve the book, his elbow hit the globe below him and knocked it off its base. It tumbled to the floor and crashed into the open bottle of bourbon that sat on the rug beside Riley's chair. The whole world, with a small dent in Asia now, rolled to Riley's feet, rolled across a spilled bottle of bourbon, spilled by his son.

Coyle's father's rage was both predictable and unpredictable. It was always there, simmering beneath the surface. Two more glasses of bourbon and he would have been too drunk to care. Two less and he would not have been drunk enough. Coyle had limped around this balance all his life and on this night, Riley Redd was in a perfect state of drunkenness.

On this night, Riley Redd jumped out of his chair and grabbed his son by the arm and there they were again. Coyle lying on the ground beneath the pole lamp, the dirt around him raised by the belt flailing on his back and Riley standing above him, roaring drunk and screaming, "You stupid boy! When are you ever going to grow up?"

Lydia had followed them, her hands fluttering against her husband's arms as always. "Now, Riley. Honey. I know he didn't mean to." Now she stood a few feet away with her arms folded tightly across her chest, as if to protect what might be inside. Coyle couldn't imagine what that might be.

He focused on her shoes. He prayed for China to start sweeping her porch and stared at his mother's tiny ankles above the black patent-leather shoes. He watched her feet shift back and forth with the slight weight of her. He watched the dust settle across the tops of her shoes and he imagined the next day when they would be sitting on a layer of newspaper just inside the kitchen door, and there would be a note on the counter that said, "China, These need to be cleaned and polished."

Coyle was lying there, watching his mother's shoes and thinking about seeing them in China's hands as she buffed across their toes with a soft yellow cloth, thinking about his mother's shoes and praying to China's porch light, and it surprised even him when he rolled over and grabbed the belt out of the air. He gave it one fierce yank and pulled his father over.

Coyle found himself standing there, feeling the weight of the belt in his hands. Riley threw his arm across his face and Coyle felt his mother's hands ripple across his arms. He heard her say, "No. No. Coyle, no. That's not how we raised you."

Coyle stood there in the light of the pole lamp. He stood frozen, the arm holding the belt up in the air and ready to strike. He could feel his father's initials in the buckle. He could have let them come crashing down. It was all he could do to keep them from crashing down.

The only movement was his mother and she fluttered between them, going first to Coyle and then to Riley and then to Coyle again until finally Coyle pushed her away, just as his father had always done.

He heard Riley whimper one drunken little whine. He saw him ease his arm down from his face and that's when Coyle started laughing. He snapped the belt in the air and watched his father cringe.

His mother lay on the ground where she'd fallen and she said, "No, Coyle. No. We didn't raise you this way."

Coyle laughed again. From across the road he heard a door slam. It was a sound from far away, like a tunnel was inside his head. It slammed again and all of them looked down the driveway towards the house across the road. China had turned her outside light on and was sweeping the porch, furiously swiping the bristles of the broom across the buckled floorboards, puffs of dust erupting at her feet.

Coyle turned and looked at his father still lying there. He threw the belt onto the ground and stalked away. He could hear Lydia sobbing behind him and if he had turned around to look, he could have seen her crawl across the grass towards her husband and he could have seen Riley push her away. He didn't turn around to look, but it was a scene as familiar to him as the glass doorknobs inside Roseberry or the faces of his ancestors' portraits hanging along the staircase wall. He could have seen it with his own eyes closed. She used to crawl that way towards him when he was lying on the ground.

Coyle didn't know where he was going. At the end of the driveway, he gazed across the road towards China's house. The porch light was off now but the parlor light was on. He didn't know that China was standing there, as dark as the shadows she huddled against. He didn't know that the broom was still in her hands and that she stood watching as he turned to the right and headed into town.

It was a four-mile walk. Even in the night the hot pavement of the highway sucked at his feet. Cars slid by but didn't stop. In town he wandered deserted streets and watched his reflection float by in the windows of shops. He watched the "Closed" signs and "We Will Be

Open Tomorrow" signs drift across the reflection of his chest. His shirt was torn. He noticed that.

He didn't know how long he wandered before a policeman picked him up.

"You're Riley Redd's son, aren't you?"

The officer shined a flashlight in his eyes and asked, "Fight with your folks?" The flashlight hovered on his face and never went down to his ripped shirt or the bruises across his arms.

Coyle nodded and climbed into the front seat of the squad car. He allowed himself to be driven back the way he'd come, down the four miles of highway to the end of the driveway at Roseberry.

The policeman dropped him off there and Coyle stood by the mailbox, listening to the tires of the squad car disappearing down the highway. He could see the orange glow of his father's cigarette on the front porch of Roseberry. He could hear him calling, "Son, is that you? Come on home now. You've upset your mother."

Coyle watched that cigarette glow and go dark, glow and go dark. He could hear his father sucking on it, could hear the rattle of ice cubes as Riley took another drink. He could hear the squeak of the chains on the porch swing as Riley sat down and called out again, "Son?"

Coyle turned away.

China found him the next morning, curled into a ball next to her front door, the broom leaning up behind him and the cat nuzzled against his leg.

It was dawn. Across the road, behind the hulking silhouette of Roseberry, the sun was brushing the sky with pink. China could see the glow of the porch light outside the kitchen door. She could see headlights coming from a long ways down the highway. Finally a car swooshed by.

China sank down and leaned against the door. She lay one hand on his back and Coyle woke up. He groaned and inched his body closer until his head lay in her lap. The cat stood up and resettled herself, turning around and bathing her toes, then falling asleep against him again. Coyle felt the callouses on China's hands moving through his hair.

Her own son was six years gone now. Earnest was six years gone and the earrings were still in Raleigh, probably sitting in plain sight on Julia's dresser and there was the child that China had seen only twice, a girl named Abolene who had just turned seven, not too long ago.

China

13

China had learned to live without Earnest. She had learned to live without knowing. She had learned to live without the earrings. She had learned to live with the coins and the watch and the key thrown into the crevice of her corner piling. China had learned to live with the constant ripple inside her heart that held her boy's name. There was nothing to be done for it.

She went to work and she came home. She turned on her porch light and swept every time Riley Redd dragged his son outside to the ground beneath the pole lamp. She baked Coyle cookies and brownies and lay her hand across his forehead and watched him grow. She polished the silver that had belonged to Beth and scrubbed the crystal that had belonged to Lula Anne. She cooked dinners and served them on Laura's favorite china. She swept cobwebs and pollen off the wide front porch of Roseberry and gazed across the street at her own empty house.

China Redd wanted her boy to come home. China Redd kept his picture in the pocket of her dress and propped it on the windowsill as she washed dishes inside Roseberry. China gazed at Earnest and wondered where he was and it was almost the same as gazing out the window at the rose garden, almost the same as gazing out the window and wondering where the kitchen house had gone, where the cabins had gone, where the bucket had gone that Cleavis had used to draw the water up with.

China wondered what had happened to her boy and the years passed. Things must have happened to mark the passing of each one of them, but all that China could think of were the letters from Julia and the pictures she sent of Abolene, growing up and looking just like Earnest when he was her age. Growing up and drawing and talking and reading just like he had. Abolene was ten years old now and China's boy had been gone for nine and each day was the same to her.

China thought that even though children were born and crops were raised and a war came and ended with their freedom, each day must have seemed the same to Cally as she waited for Cleavis. Each day must have stretched before her as gray as the slate gray of her eyes. Each day must have brought Cally that much closer to the truth that she would never see her boy again.

It was the very day that Riley Redd was killed that China decided to visit Cally and to lay her heart out to the stones upon the hillside in the old cemetery up in the woods.

It was not the white Redds' cemetery that China sought to visit, not the white Redds' cemetery with its tall wrought-iron fence and creaking gate and bulbous boxwoods spreading their growth among tombstones, its thin half-round markers with their barely visible words, its tiny lambs for the children who had died after Cally stole the earrings. It was not the white Redds' cemetery with its thick marble slabs showing the names and dates of people that China had worked for.

China walked past the white Redds' cemetery without knowing that in three days' time there would be a freshly dug grave. In three days' time there would be a mound of dirt covered with a green plastic tarp and a blue tent and a bank of flowers and a double tombstone with Riley's name on one side and the other side blank and waiting for his wife, Lydia.

China walked past that wrought-iron gate and the scent of the boxwoods and into the place where the trail narrowed, into the woods along a pine-needled path, into a clearing with rows and rows of upturned rocks.

Cally was buried here. Tom and Tuly too. China knew which rocks belonged to them. It was passed down to her, the same as the snuffbox of earrings, passed down to her the same as the piece of Cally's head rag, passed down to her the same as the story that grew and grew. China knew which rocks belonged to Cally and Tom and Tuly, even though she didn't know the names of the other rocks inside that clearing. There were nineteen in all, and China didn't know if they were men or women or children. China didn't have little lambs to go by or a gardener who tended the grounds or double tombstones where wives were buried next to husbands. China knew which rocks belonged to Cally and Tom and Tuly, even though they weren't buried side by side.

Tom had died first and the rock that marked his grave was in the third row, second to the right. Tuly had died next. It was a fever that killed her, China's daddy had said, and she was also in the third row, three stones down. Then Cally died, living another three years without Tom or Tuly or Cleavis. Cally was buried in the very front row, all the way to the right. Cally was the last one buried in the unmarked plot on the top of the hill.

It was a Sunday when China decided to visit Cally and pour her heart out to the clearing of rocks, to try to explain why the earrings weren't where they should have been and to pray to God and whoever might listen to send them back to her. At least the earrings, China thought, and Earnest might follow. At least the earrings and after that her boy might come home.

It was a Sunday when China tucked the worn-thin picture of Earnest into the pocket of her dress and crossed the highway and climbed the hill behind Roseberry. It was a Sunday and China had awakened from a dream at 2 A.M. and had lain there in bed staring at the ceiling and waiting for the sun to rise.

China had had this dream before. It was the dream where Earnest was a boy again and was reaching under the house for the earrings and he was dangling them in the light when Riley Redd turned the corner. China had had this dream before and she always woke from it at 2 A.M. and when she did she always waited. That's the way it was on the day that Riley Redd died. It was a waiting day. First she waited in bed for the sun to rise, and then she waited on the porch with the thin yellow blanket tucked around her legs, and then she waited for her eggs to boil and her coffee to brew. China stood on the faint brown patch on the kitchen floor and listened to the plunking of the percolator and the rattling of the eggs against the sides of the pan on the stove. China waited and wondered what to do today, on Sunday, her day off. It was standing on her birth spot that China decided to visit the graveyard.

Because it was Sunday, there was more waiting after breakfast. China did not want to see the white Redds so she waited for them to leave for church. She waited to hear the car doors slamming and the engine starting up and to see the Buick sliding out onto the highway.

When the car disappeared, China Redd pulled on her old brown jacket and picked up the broom leaning against the wall of the porch. She headed down the lane towards Roseberry. She scuffed through the dry, fallen oak leaves in the driveway. She walked past the house, past Mamie's wisteria, past the back porch where the key was kept on a string suspended from the light fixture, past the rose garden that China used to gaze at before she started gazing at the soft, worn picture of Earnest.

China crossed the field. She walked past the piles of rocks laid there by the field hands clearing the land, rocks now partially hidden by the high, weedy grasses of Chatham County. China kicked at one when she went by.

She walked past the tumble of logs that had once been cabins. She walked up the rutted carriage trail that led into the woods. She walked across the bridge that spanned the Haw River, up the hill and past the white Redds' cemetery.

China Redd walked along the narrow trail and into the clearing and she drifted between the rows of rocks. She lay her hand on each and every one of them. She stopped at the one that was Cally's and said, "I don't have the earrings anymore. They're gone and so is my boy."

China Redd pulled the picture out of her pocket and stared into Earnest's eyes.

"Listen to me," China said to the wind. "Listen to me. I know what it is to lose your boy."

China picked up sticks and stones and tossed them into the woods. She took the broom and swept the ground clean between the rows of rocks and left it leaning against a cedar tree. As she was walking home and crossing the muddy brown waters of the Haw River, China Redd heard the singing from the white folk's church, drifting up the hill and settling in the tops of the trees like a flock of birds.

It was that afternoon that Riley Redd got drunk and went barreling across the field on the old blue tractor and hit that pile of rocks left there by the field hands and now partially hidden in the high weeds. It was the same old blue tractor that Riley had torn down the cabins with, and when it hit the rocks it flipped over and killed him.

China saw it. She had been brought outside by the noise of the tractor. She saw him heading for that mound of rocks hidden in the grass. China Redd was about to say, "Look out," but he wouldn't have heard her and by then it was too late. The tractor was on its side and China saw it lying there with its front wheel spinning.

There had been a day that China remembered, a day when China was young and her mother had taken her to the clearing where Cally and Tom were buried.

Earnestine had been working in her garden that day,

clearing new land and pulling rocks out of the soil, tossing them into a pile at the edge of the fence.

When they were walking home from the graveyard, they had crossed the very field that Riley Redd died in and they had stopped to rest on that very pile of rocks and watch the sunset. China could remember her mother running calloused hands across the rock that she sat on and she could remember her mother saying, "I never seen such a rocky place as Chatham County. It's downright unfriendly."

There was no love lost, as far as China was concerned. Riley Redd was mean from the get-go. China could remember mouthing those very words to Earnest when he was a boy.

There was no love lost when Riley Redd died, but, as with every death in Roseberry, there was work to be done. There was the house to be cleaned to a spit polish for the after-funeral gathering of townsfolk. There were the casseroles and pies and Jell-O salads arriving at the front door. There was the large coffee urn to clean and bring into service, the plates to be stacked, utensils to be laid out, cups and saucers to be balanced across the top of the buffet in the dining room.

There was no love lost when Riley Redd died, but there was a lot of work to be done and China did it. The house was cleaned from top to bottom. Coyle's suit was pressed and laid across his bed. Casseroles were warmed in the oven. Cakes were laid across the shining mahogany of the dining-room table.

China stood at the dining-room window and watched Riley Redd's funeral procession cross the back driveway and proceed along the newly made road that ran across the field.

The new road had been made in a hurry, gravel dumped and spread in a path across the sharp, high grasses, past the pile of rocks that had turned over Riley Redd's tractor, and along the rutted carriage trail leading to the white Redds' cemetery. Even trees had to be cut down and a parking lot made in the woods to accommodate the cars.

"The cars have to have a place to turn around," Lydia had said. "It's been so long since we've had a death in this family that I'm afraid we've let things go a bit too much up there."

So trees were cut down and hauled out of sight. Stumps were wrenched out of the ground and dumptruck-loads of dirt brought in to fill in the holes. Gravel was spread and George was sent to the graveyard to rake the leaves and trim the grass and shape up the boxwoods. At the last minute China was sent there to scrub the green moss off the little stone bench.

George drove her up in his truck, the wheels sinking into the thick layer of gravel and China's bucket and brushes and gallon jugs of hot soapy water riding in the back.

The new parking lot was complete. The trees had been hauled out of sight and the holes filled in and the gravel laid. Riley Redd's grave was dug and the green tarp covered the mound of dirt and a blue tent was set up and a headstone rested in place.

China creaked the gate open and stepped inside. She knelt beside the little stone bench, close to the grave of

William Lars Redd and she scraped a bit of moss off the feet of it and then dipped her brush in and began scrubbing.

Behind her, she could hear George picking up branches and raking leaves. Above her, she could hear the shrill call of a hawk. All around her, she could hear the dead brown leaves rattling and falling into the woods.

China poured a gallon of rinse water across the top of the bench and stood up. Stone benches in cemeteries are supposed to have moss growing on them, China thought. It's just one more thing for me to clean.

When she turned around she was facing the new parking lot and, with the trees cut down and the view opened up, the clearing of rocks that China had visited on the day that Riley Redd died was clearly visible. China could see Cally's rock, with the small spray of wildflowers she had left there. She could see Tuly's rock and Tom's rock and all the rocks in-between. She could see the freshly swept ground with the brush strokes of the broom across the dirt. She could see her own broom leaning there against a cedar tree.

Right there was the story of the earrings, the people who stole them and kept them hidden, the man who could sigh such a coldness that it would circle Roseberry like wind and chill white people into the marrow of their bones.

There was a cold wind such as that on the day that Riley Redd was buried. China stood at the dining-room window and watched the funeral procession cross the driveway and move along the newly made road across the field. China watched the row of shiny cars pass the rose garden and go between the barns and beside the pile of rocks and past the tumbled-down logs that had once been cabins. China saw the leaves scudding across the grass. China held her hand to the glass in the window above Mamie's wisteria and she felt the coldness of the day outside.

Coyle

14

Coyle Redd was sixteen years old when his father died. For three years he had tiptoed around Roseberry without a beating but expecting one every day. And it was almost worse after Riley died, after Coyle saw his father's mangled body carried from the field to the back porch of Roseberry, after the wake and the funeral and even after the graveside service.

Long after Riley Redd died driving the tractor too fast across the field, his son's muscles would tense every time he dropped something or made a noise, every time he slipped through the dining room into the kitchen for his breakfast, every time he saw his father's empty chair. They tensed at the sight of Riley Redd's picture along the staircase wall.

After his father died, Coyle Redd felt the house whispering to him. He felt Roseberry pulsing like it had a heartbeat of its own. He had dreams about the ground next to his father's grave where his mother would lie. He had dreams about the ground next to her grave where he would lie.

Coyle's muscles tensed at the sound of ice cubes hitting the bottom of a mason jar as China poured herself some tea, at the sound of George's clippers outside the dining-room window, at the sound of Lydia opening a newspaper and snapping the pages in the air.

At the same time, Lydia Redd's muscles loosened. Coyle could see it in her face, even standing in the cemetery on the hill on the day his father was buried, surrounded by mourners and the wrought-iron fence, listening to words like, "Fine and upstanding." "Prominent and generous." "Heritage and backbone."

Coyle listened to the word "tragic," the word "God" and the word "loss," and he saw something ease in his mother's face. As the casket was lowered he saw lines disappear. As Lydia threw the first handful of dirt across the shiny, dark wood-and-brass trim of the coffin, Coyle saw her shoulders loosen and drop and soften. After Riley Redd died, Lydia started sitting on the couch with her bare feet curled under her like a schoolgirl. She leaned back into the upholstery. She never sat on the edge anymore. She never wound her legs together like a hard-baked pretzel and she never clenched her mouth into a tightly packed line and she never picked up her embroidery, jamming the needle into the cloth and pulling the thread through.

The sounds of Riley raising a glass to his lips and of Lydia running thread through cloth were replaced by a new sound. The sound was of a pen scratching across paper and later, from Riley's den, the sound of typewriter keys being pecked and paper being zipped out of the carriage. Lydia Redd was writing a book.

The book was published the next year under the title *The Legends of Roseberry*. It was published by a university press and Lydia shelved a copy in the den and signed one for Coyle and another for China and then she threw herself a party.

China worked that party. Coyle watched her carry salads and casseroles and plates of sliced ham into the dining room. He watched her arrange celery sticks and carrot sticks and pieces of fruit on glass trays. He watched her stack cups and saucers and spread out spoons and forks and knives and napkins.

Roseberry filled with guests and local reporters and photographers. Lydia led her son around the parlor and introduced him to the daughters of her friends. Lydia would whisper into his ear, "She's your age," or, "I think you'll get along with this one. She's very charming."

Lydia Redd was doing what any upstanding mother from a good family would do: she was shopping. She was trying to find suitable girls for her son to date. She was trying to steer him in the direction that a young man needed to be steered in. She was trying to help him connect to good stock.

Coyle had heard of good stock before. Coyle knew that there were girls you dated and girls you married and girls you used. He had known it all along, but he had learned it again a few years earlier when he got into a fight at school over a girl named Jenny Wolfe.

Coyle had been watching Jenny Wolfe since grade school. He knew that she was one of the ones you used. He had seen her mother down at the Piggly Wiggly, checking groceries. He had seen her walking along the highway carrying brown paper bags.

Even in grade school Coyle knew that a boy like him could never date a girl like Jenny Wolfe, a girl with only one parent, a girl with only one parent who didn't even have a car. A girl like that didn't have what his mother called "prospects." A girl like that was not what his parents called "good stock." A girl like that could never be brought home to meet Lydia Redd. Even in grade school Coyle knew this.

All the same, he watched her. He even stole things from her, pencils and yarn from her scarf and a mitten. He stole these things and kept them under his pillow and felt them at night while he slept. In the morning, before China came upstairs to make the beds, he hid them in the drawer of his nightstand. They were still there.

Coyle had watched Jenny Wolfe for a long time and when her body suddenly burst out into an awkward version of womanhood, other boys started watching her too. That was how the fight began.

It was in the cafeteria, and another boy had reached out and pinched one of Jenny Wolfe's breasts as she walked by. Coyle had heard her tray of food clatter across the floor. He had seen the hot squash casserole clinging to her stockings and burning tiny blisters into the skin of her ankles. He had seen Jenny Wolfe's hands go up to the roundness of her chest.

Before he knew what he was doing, Coyle was pounding the boy's head against the hard brown linoleum. He heard shouting going on around him and felt hands on his back, tugging at his shirt and trying to pull him off.

Coyle landed in detention and the boy he had beaten

landed in the emergency room, getting nine stitches across the wound at the back of his head.

Jenny Wolfe never said a word to either one of them. She left the cafeteria and went to the bathroom and laid wet paper towels across the fiery pinpricks on her ankles. She let Coyle serve his time in detention without a word. She shuddered when she saw the partially shaved head and the ghastly stitches zigzagging their way across the scalp of the boy who had pinched her.

She stayed clear of both of them until she heard that Coyle's father had died and then she went up to him after school one day and laid her hand on his sleeve and said simply, "I'm sorry about your father. My dad's dead too." And she walked away.

Coyle could remember his father standing beside the fireplace in the living room the night after the fight in the cafeteria. He could see Riley leaning one elbow on the mantel, a blaze crackling on the hearth below. A log rolled out and as Riley nudged it back in with his foot, he said, "A fight? My boy in a fight? Why?"

Coyle told him and Riley started laughing.

"You landed him in the emergency room? Well, I tell you, Son, it's good. Every kind of woman needs her honor defended," he said. "Just don't go marrying her."

Coyle's mother sat on the couch with her legs crossed at the ankles, her hair pulled into a tight bun, her hands clasped together in her lap and her head bowed. She looked up when Riley said this and then she looked down again.

"Well, that's right isn't it, Lydia? You marry good stock. Right, Honey? Like you. You're good stock."

There was something in his father's voice that Coyle didn't understand. He only knew that it was sharp and mean and that it had something to do with his mother sitting on the couch with her legs twined at the ankles.

Riley knelt down and picked up the poker and jabbed it into the fire, stirring sparks up the chimney. Later on that night he climbed the stairs and knocked on Coyle's door and stepped inside.

Riley said, "Son, I don't want you to go getting all googley over this Jenny Wolfe girl. I'm sure she's a looker and a real sweet gal, flattered as hell that you put up for her, but she's got to understand one thing. It means nothing to you." Riley waved his hands through the air. "Any gentleman would have done the same thing.

"You've got to have someone who understands you," Riley continued. "That's all I'm saying. You got to hook up with a woman who understands you."

"Does Mother understand you?" Coyle asked.

"Perfectly," Riley replied. "Just perfectly." He shut the door and the latch clicked into place.

It was after his mother's party that Coyle decided to slip a note to Jenny Wolfe. It was after *The Legends of Roseberry* was published, after Lydia had led him around the parlor of Roseberry, introducing him to the daughters of her friends, each one of these girls holding out her properly gloved hand, each one of them well-bred enough to ask him more questions about himself than he could ever want to answer, each one of them small and slight and wispy and more insipid than the last.

Coyle had slipped through the kitchen and out the

back door, holding one finger to his lips, asking China not to tell. He had sneaked across the field, past the rocks that had killed his father. He had sat down on one of the rotten logs of the torn-down cabins and he had decided to pen a note to Jenny Wolfe, and even after he had decided, he continued to sit there.

He watched the guests leave one by one. He watched his mother wave and smile and grasp hands and look into people's eyes. He watched the sun set and the lights inside Roseberry come on. He watched China standing at the window washing dishes and then finally stepping out the back door to leave. He watched the beam of China's flashlight bobbing along the lane towards home.

15

It was May when Coyle passed the note to Jenny Wolfe. The leaves were out and the sap had risen and Coyle asked Jenny to meet him after school in back of the old Tastee Freeze.

The old Tastee Freeze was along the highway, just beyond the Piggly Wiggly where Jenny's mother worked. It was a small, abandoned brick building with a glass front and plastic signs still hanging in the windows. The colors on the signs were faded from the sun. The hamburger had taken on a greenish hue. The pickle was yellow. The cones of swirled ice cream were a washed-out white.

The pavement of the parking lot was cracked and tufted with weeds. Princess trees had broken through the asphalt and grew along the sides of the building, hugging the bricks with their large green leaves. A stack of old rubber mats sat outside the back door, cracked and twined with a honeysuckle vine that was thick with the scent of white and yellow flowers.

Coyle and Jenny lay side by side on the pavement next to the rubber mats. Coyle liked the feel of the warm black-top through his clothing. He liked the feel of the warmth of their shoulders just barely touching.

Jenny shaded her eyes with one arm flung over her face.

"Tell me things," she said.

"What sort of things?" Coyle asked.

"Things," she said. "Tell me about the house you live in. It's big. Tell me which room is yours."

They spent two weeks meeting every afternoon when school let out, lying on the pavement in back of the old Tastee Freeze, Jenny shading her eyes and asking Coyle questions.

What were his mother's parties like? What was the food like? Did China serve him breakfast, lunch and dinner? How was the house furnished? Where were the portraits of his ancestors hung? Was there really a vine called Mamie's wisteria?

Coyle enjoyed the questions. It saved him from trying to think of something to say. He lay on the warm pavement and felt Jenny's shoulder brushing up against his and listened and answered.

He drew a map of Roseberry and its grounds in a pool

of gritty dirt that had blown against the building. He used a stick to trace the back door that China entered and exited every day, the den where his father had sat, the parlor where his mother had sewn, the staircase where the portraits hung, the hallway of rooms upstairs, the tiny door that led to the attic. He traced the rose garden and the barns and the fields and the old slave cabins. Finally he traced the new road and the parking lots and the cemetery where his father was buried.

Coyle gave Jenny his copy of his mother's book and she read it all in one night, propped up in her bed with the lamp on. When they met again she sank down beside the rubber mats and clutched the book against her chest.

"It's so romantic," she proclaimed.

"What is?" Coyle asked.

"Roseberry. The house you live in."

"Don't take it to heart," Coyle said. He sat down and stretched his body alongside of hers. He nestled his shoulder close to Jenny's shoulder. "Mother left a few things out," he said. "She left out Bessie."

"Who's Bessie?"

"Bessie Redd," Coyle answered. "Jennis Redd's younger sister. She was staying with Lula Anne towards the end of the war and, before it was all over, she'd run off with a Yankee soldier and my family never forgave her. We scratched her name out of the Bible and took her portrait off the staircase wall. They completely erased her. China had to tell me who she was. You won't find her in there." Coyle thumped the book that Jenny held.

"They erased her?"

"Erased her completely. Tried to anyway. I found her portrait up in the attic." Coyle chuckled to himself. "I used to pray to her," he said.

"Pray to Bessie?"

"I was young," Coyle said. "I propped her picture up on top of a trunk draped with an old scarf and surrounded her with dead flowers and lit candles and I prayed to Bessie. I nearly set the house on fire and when Riley found out. . . ."

Coyle didn't finish. It wasn't he who had caused that fire. It wasn't he but his father and Coyle wasn't ready to tell that to Jenny. He wasn't ready to tell Jenny about the yard under the pole lamp and the way the dirt would rise and the grass would be whipped apart in clumps. He wasn't ready to tell Jenny about the belt or seeing his father's initials stamped in bruises across his flesh. He wasn't ready to tell Jenny about China sweeping her porch at night or about the stock of brand-new shirts that hung stiffly in his closet and the way that the old ones, the ones that were torn and ripped and sometimes crusted with blood, would just disappear.

Coyle knew it was his mother who had taken them, that she sneaked into his room on the mornings after a beating and that she picked up his torn shirts and carried them away somewhere, carried them away to some mysterious place, carried them away before China could get upstairs to make the beds.

Coyle had looked for them once. He had checked his mother's closet and the trunk of her car. He had checked beneath the house and the barrel out back where George burned the trash. He had scraped through the ashes looking for a button or a scrap of plaid cloth or a label from inside a collar.

Coyle had looked in the attic. He had peered into boxes and the drawers of old bureaus. He had looked behind the old Victrola and in the trousseaus of ladies long dead. He had looked behind the trunk where Bessie's portrait was still crammed. Crammed there with an oval of broken glass. Crammed there after Riley had found him praying to Bessie.

It had not been Coyle who nearly set the house on fire. Coyle was always careful with the candles. He had set them inside of old saucers with chipped edges. He had glued them there by their own melted wax.

It had been Riley who nearly burned the house down, who had upset the candles after stepping into the attic and hearing Coyle muttering his prayer to the portrait of Bessie Redd.

"Please, Bessie, get me out of here."

It was hearing that prayer that had made Riley grab his son by the collar and fling him to his feet. It was hearing that prayer and snatching Coyle up too quickly that had made the candles turn over and set the scarf on fire.

The stain of black soot was still there, still rising in a dark smudge up the eaves of the attic. The ashes of the scarf were still there, too, ground into the floor where the slaves once slept.

But it was his mother who had told him about the house slaves sleeping in the attic, who explained to him that it was the feet of the house slaves going up and down the stairs that had worn the treads into scooped-out hollow bowls.

He was very young then and he had watched her lay one hand inside the hollow of a stair tread. He had listened to her tell him that there had been quilts hanging for walls in the middle of the room and that the slaves had made pallets on the floor. Coyle had asked, "What is a pallet?"

This was before he had started school, before he had made his altar to Bessie, before the black sooty stain had appeared on the eaves of the attic. He was very young then, but even so there were bruises across his back from his father's belt.

His mother had taken him to the attic because it was raining, because he couldn't go outside and he was bored, because he had been whining about it while Lydia sat on the couch and worked her embroidery. Finally, Lydia had laid down her sewing and grabbed his shirtsleeve.

"I have something to show you," she said.

She marched him up the stairs past the baleful eyes of the ancestors' portraits, down the hallway and into the narrow staircase with the worn and bowled steps and up into the humid air of the attic. The rain was heavy on the roof and Lydia had to shout to be heard over the din of it.

"Be thankful that you're white," she yelled. "And that you were born into a good family."

"What's a pallet?" Coyle shouted back.

"It's a bed."

"Why isn't it called a bed?"

"It's a makeshift bed."

"From what?"

"From blankets and quilts. Whatever they could find."

"Didn't they have real beds?"

"It was how they wanted it," his mother said.

"Does China sleep in a real bed?"

Lydia laughed. "I don't know what China does," she answered.

The next day Coyle asked China if she slept in a real bed or on a pallet on the floor and she cocked her head at him and said, "What are you asking a question such as that for?"

Coyle shrugged. He lowered his head and told her about the slaves in the attic, how his mother had said they made pallets for their beds, how she had said it was how they wanted it.

"Slaves didn't have much choice about where to make their beds," China replied. "And anyway, I'm not a slave. I sleep in a bed. I sleep in a wrought-iron bed that belonged to my momma and daddy."

Coyle did not tell these things to Jenny while lying on the pavement in back of the old Tastee Freeze. Instead he shook his head and let a little laugh out into the spring air and said, "Bessie's the only one of us not buried up on that hill."

"She's buried somewhere," Jenny said. A crow flew across the sky, cawing loudly. There were clouds gathering in the west, down the highway, down the road where Roseberry was.

"I have to go," Coyle said.

He never met Jenny behind the old Tastee Freeze again. He was relieved when he heard that she was pregnant by a vet named Bets Monroe, a guy who lived in his father's garden shed. He didn't need a girl like that in his life, Coyle told himself.

Jenny Wolfe dropped out of school.

China

16

There were pictures in the book that Lydia Redd gave to China. Pictures that China had never seen before. Pictures that were not the scaled-down reproductions of the family portraits that headed every chapter and marched through the book the same way that they marched along the staircase wall from downstairs to upstairs. Those pictures, those portraits stepped from Rose Redd all the way through to Coyle.

But these pictures that China had never seen before began with Jennis and Lula Anne and William Lars Redd. These pictures were truer than the paintings. They were reproductions of photographs, photographs that must have been tucked away somewhere inside Roseberry, tucked into a place that China had never been before, tucked into a place that didn't need cleaning or dusting or folding or polishing. It was hard for China to imagine that such a place existed.

The first picture was a faded photograph of Jennis Redd. China was sitting at the kitchen table inside Roseberry when she first saw it. She leaned forward and studied Jennis. She leaned forward and tried to imagine his features on the face of a boy who got sold away the day after he was drawing water from the well. She leaned forward and studied the hands that had touched Cally, the hands of the man who was father to Cleavis.

In the picture Jennis Redd was standing beside a chair, wearing the uniform of a Confederate officer. A saber was dangling from his waist and drawing across his leg. Jennis Redd's chin was raised and covered with a pointy beard and whiskers. He looked sternly into the camera, one hand tucked inside his belt and the other resting on his chest.

China studied those hands, the hands that had once or twice or more touched Cally, the hands that must have given the earrings to his wife, the hands that had once signed papers and made lists and kept records for the plantation called Roseberry. China studied those hands. She studied the eyes. She studied the picture as a whole.

There were lines across the picture, lines that had once been creases in the original photograph and China wondered if Lula Anne had kept this picture close to her while Jennis was gone. China wondered if Lula Anne had slept with it under her pillow with her hand resting on it, the same way that China had taken to doing with Earnest's picture, sleeping with it and carrying it with her all the time, propping it on the window ledge of the sink as she washed the white Redds' dishes, propping it on the table as she sprinkled flour and rolled out biscuit dough, picking it up to gaze into Earnest's eyes every now and then and leaving a floury thumbprint on the bottom corner, a mother's thumbprint that brushed across the lapel of young Earnest's jacket.

China wondered if Lula Anne missed Jennis as badly as Cally had missed Cleavis and if so, how? How could a woman miss a man like that, knowing that he took nightly walks down to the cabins to knock on Cally's door? How could a woman miss a man who fathered his own property? How could a woman believe that a house like Roseberry could keep her warm when there were sighs like Tom's circling all across Chatham County? China wondered if Lula Anne hated the pointed whiskers on his chin.

China wondered if Lula Anne had not crumpled her fist around this picture of Jennis one night, wadded it and thrown it across the room, maybe when she thought of a boy drawing water from a well, maybe when she thought of the features of her husband on that boy's face, maybe when she thought of her own earrings in the palm of that boy's hand.

There was a second picture with Jennis in it. It was a picture of the three of them, Jennis and Lula Anne and William Lars Redd. In this second picture, Jennis was wearing the same uniform and Lula Anne was sitting in the same chair that had previously been empty. Lula Anne's dark dress was spread all around her and her hands rested in the folds of her lap. William Lars Redd was wearing shorts and suspenders and leaning against his momma's knee. William Lars Redd looked like he must have been only four or five years old.

China looked into the eyes of William Lars Redd. His face was as young and sweet-looking as any young face could be. His hand rested lightly on his mother's knee. His head leaned towards her the way a young child's would.

China looked into the eyes of Lula Anne, into the hardness of them, into the lines that spread from their rims, into the slash of mouth that crossed her face, into the white line of scalp that parted her hair.

There was something else that China saw that day as she sat at the kitchen table at Roseberry and gazed into the picture that she had never seen before. There was something else that China saw in that picture of Lula Anne Redd, something that made her steal an antique magnifying glass and carry it home in the pocket of her dress.

China had never stolen anything from Roseberry before that night, nothing more than leftovers and the almost-empty ends of toilet paper spools. But China knew that this was stealing, even as she slid the magnifying glass from the drawer of Riley's desk, even as she slid the fancy glass into the plain pocket of her dress. China knew that this was stealing and the thing that made her do it was the pair of abalone earrings, peeking out from the sweeps of hair that covered the tops of Lula Anne's ears.

The stolen magnifying glass inside her pocket bumped against China's leg as she packaged up the leftover party food to take home with her. It bumped against China's leg as she followed the beam of her flashlight down the driveway, carrying the copy of the book that Lydia had inscribed for her.

"For China, Our special friend here at Roseberry. Fondly, Mrs. Riley Redd."

China sat at her own kitchen table with the bare light-bulb hanging from its black cord like a tiny moon, shining its thin, harsh light down onto the pages of Lydia Redd's book. China held the glass and peered through it at Lula Anne's ears, unmistakably the teardrops of seashell, unmistakably the earrings that Cleavis once held in his hand, unmistakably the earrings that Cally wrapped in cotton and cloth, unmistakably the earrings that her boy, Earnest, had carried out of Chatham County.

China ran the glass across Lula Anne's face, across the face of Jennis with his pointy beard, each hair magnified, coarse and cruel. China ran the glass across the face of William Lars Redd, across the suspenders he wore, across his hand resting lightly on his mother's knee.

China Redd could feel her hand tremble. She could feel the earrings all the stronger in their goneness. She could see them dangling against the cocoa-brown skin of her mother's long neck. She could feel the way that they lay in the pink of her palm when she took them from Earnest and put them back where they belonged.

Earnest was always crawling under the house and pulling the snuffbox out of the crevice in the corner piling and China remembered it all with a clarity that shook her. The scrape of the metal against the rocks, the swirls of color, some blue, some green, some gray like the slate of Cally's eyes, the faded gold trim shaped into two tears, the flakes of rust falling off the snuffbox and the dry, rotted cloth of Cally's head rag and the scruff of field cotton that they nestled in. China could remember these things, sitting at her kitchen table holding a stolen magnifying glass across the picture of Jennis and Lula Anne and William Lars Redd.

The date below the picture said "1861." It was a picture taken the very year that Cleavis was sold and China could imagine a jaunt into town in the carriage, a black driver, fields that were being worked by people with nothing of their own unless they stole it. China could imagine Cally and Tom out in the field, hearing the rattle of the carriage as it swept by along the old trail through the woods. China could imagine them leaning over, working, hoeing or picking cotton with long cloth bags slung across their shoulders and dragging the ground between the rows. China could imagine the gray of Callie's eyes and the growing roundness of her stomach. China could imagine Callie's fingers bleeding from the scratch of seeds and pods, just as her own had bled as they searched the rocks for the snuffbox that held Cally's earrings.

China Redd had been calling her son's wife lately, begging Julia to send the earrings back home and then stopping herself and saying, "No, let me come get them. I'll take a few days off. They won't be safe in the mail."

It had been ten years now since Earnest disappeared and Julia had been telling China to move on from it, as if a mother could move on from a child. Julia should know that. Any mother should know that. It's just not possible.

Julia had been telling China to move on from it and that the earrings belonged to Abolene now. Julia had been telling China that they were all that Abolene had of her daddy, besides her name and her looks.

"She's keeping them," Julia had said. "She's keeping them."

Julia had been telling China to move on and that it didn't matter anyway. Julia had been telling China that the earrings weren't going to bring Earnest home.

Abolene

17

Abolene arrived by bus. She arrived in June, three months after her mother died. She arrived wearing a button and a wedding ring on a string around her neck. Abolene Redd arrived carrying a wooden box of paints in her lap and hauling a suitcase heavy with grief and fear and the clothes of a young girl. Her momma was dead and there was nothing that could change that.

Abolene Redd turned twelve years old on the very day that Julia was buried. Her Aunt Louisa said it was the angels that came and took her momma in the dead of night but the doctors said it was a heart murmur. Folks around town said it was a blessing for a soul to leave this world so swiftly and painlessly and the preacher said that Julia Redd must have been living right. But Abolene's Aunt Dee said that Julia Redd just got lucky, because she never went to church.

Three days before Abolene arrived in Chatham County she had been sitting on her mother's four-poster bed in their basement apartment, listening to her Uncle Silo sell the furniture in the next room. She was sitting there watching her aunts go through her mother's closet, looking for a dress to take to the funeral home.

"Death gets busy," Aunt Louisa had said, swiping the metal coat hangers across the closet rod.

Dee punched her sister on the arm and rolled her eyes towards Abolene.

Louisa corrected herself. "There's so much to do," she said.

It was March and the dogwood outside Julia's bedroom window was just beginning to bud. Every year for as long as Abolene could remember, her mother had taken her outside during the last week of February. Julia would take Abolene's hand and fold her fingers around the end of a stem on the dogwood tree and Abolene would feel the tiny bulge of a bud underneath the waxy layer of bark.

"Can you feel it?" Julia asked and Abolene would nod yes. She could feel it, she would say. "It's the promise of spring," her mother told her.

This year had been no different. It was just the week before her momma died that Abolene had felt the promise of spring with her hand wrapped around that dogwood tree.

Louisa was holding up a white chiffon dress now. Abolene called it her mother's cloud dress. Julia had liked to wear it when she went dancing with her boyfriend, a mechanic named Joe Skinner. Aunt Dee was shaking her head no to this dress.

"Absolutely not," she said. "No, no, no."

Abolene wanted to go live with Joe Skinner but that's not what Dee and Louisa had decided for her. Dee and Louisa had decided that she should go to live with her grandmother in Chatham County. They couldn't take her in, they both said. Their houses were full.

Abolene could not remember Gramma China except as a voice on the telephone and a ten-dollar bill tucked inside of birthday cards. She had just gotten one of China's birthday cards. It said, "Now You Are Twelve," and was bordered with pink roses. It lay beside her on the bed. It was mailed the day before her momma died.

It was Joe Skinner who Abolene had called that morning, the morning that she couldn't wake her momma and had shaken her and shaken her and called her and called her but Julia just lay there. She didn't look right. She didn't feel right, either.

Joe had been Julia's boyfriend for two years now. Abolene didn't even know the numbers for her aunts but she knew Joe's numbers, both the garage and the apartment above it, where he lived.

When Joe got Abolene's call, he had dropped the receiver so that it was left dangling against the yellow kitchen wall of his apartment. He lived two blocks away and he ran the entire distance, even though there were plenty of cars to drive.

He ran across yards and past barking dogs and women in bathrobes picking up morning papers. He jumped freshly planted gardens and hedges of boxwoods. When Abolene opened the door for him he rushed into Julia's room and shook her and said her name over and over again, just the same way that Abolene had done. Then he called 911, but it was too late.

It was Joe who told Abolene her momma was dead. He

didn't know the right way to say it and he couldn't believe it himself. In the end he just pulled her to him and said, "Abby, your momma's passed away." His voice choked up but he got the words out and then he held her and called Julia's sisters.

Abolene sat in his lap while they waited. She knew that she was too old for laps but Joe had said that it was okay and he wrapped his big arms around her. She could smell the Go-Jo Grease Remover that he washed his hands with. She could feel him trying to keep himself from crying.

The armchair they sat in was the first thing sold, and it rode out of Abolene's life roped to the top of a station wagon. Uncle Silo had placed an ad in one of the papers and all day long the phone had been ringing and strangers had been coming over and haggling over the prices that he had set. Silo would lower his voice and nod towards Abolene and say, "orphan," and he would always get what he was asking. Abolene's own bed was carried off in a rust-colored pickup truck on the morning that the aunts were going through the closet.

"Keep going," Abolene heard Dee saying as Louisa scraped the coat hangers to one side.

Louisa held up a blue dress.

"Too bright?" she asked.

Dee nodded. "Much, much too bright."

Abolene loved that dress. It was the color of the sky in one of her mother's paintings. It was called periwinkle. Periwinkle blue.

Both Dee and Louisa thought painting was foolish. They thought it was child's play and that Julia should have given all her paints to Abolene and started living like a grown-up.

That's how Dee had put it. She said it one day recently, on one of her rare visits, before Julia died. She also said that Joe Skinner ought to marry Julia or else get out of the way so an honest man could get in. Julia had laughed at Dee.

"You won't find a man more honest than Joe Skinner," Julia said. "Besides, I've already been married."

Julia had given her wedding ring to Abolene. That was years ago, the same day that she had handed Abolene the earrings and told her where they had come from and that her Gramma China thought they would bring her father home and that it was all a silly story.

"Nothing will bring him home," Julia had said. "He's gone," she said, and then she slid the gold band off the finger of her left hand and said, "Here, you may as well have this too."

Abolene kept the earrings in their snuffbox on her dresser. She took them out from time to time and held them to her own lobes and looked in the mirror. She wiggled the clasps back and forth, trying to get them free of the rust that held them shut, trying to open them so that she could put them on for real. The earrings were sealed tight with age and moisture.

Abolene didn't think she would ever get to wear the pretty earrings and the wedding band was too large, even for her thumb. So Abolene kept it threaded with white string and tied around her neck. She never took it off, not even to sleep. If she was troubled she moved it back and forth across the string.

That was what she was doing while sitting on the bed next to the birthday card from Gramma China. Abolene was scooting her mother's wedding band back and forth across the string, the same way that Aunt Louisa scooted coat hangers across the closet rod.

Aunt Louisa was holding up a light pink shift now. The dress had a row of gold crimped buttons going in a straight line down the front.

"What about this one?" she asked.

"It's missing a button," Dee said, pointing.

Abolene watched as both the aunts peered down to examine the frayed empty threads. They straightened back up and turned their heads this way and that, the same way her mother had turned her head from side to side when she wasn't sure about the color in one of her paintings.

"It won't show," Louisa said. "The casket will be closed to here." She held her hand to her waist, palm facing downward.

"Shush." Dee glowered at her sister and nodded her head towards Abolene.

Abolene rose from the edge of the bed and walked over to her mother's dresser. It was really a vanity but her mother had always called it a dresser. The last thing her mother needed was a vanity. Abolene had heard Joe say that her momma was such a natural beauty that she didn't even need a mirror. Abolene wondered if she would ever be as pretty as her momma or have a boyfriend like Joe.

Now her momma was crossing over the River Jordan; that's how Dee and Louisa had put it. Her momma was crossing over the River Jordan and Abolene stood in her bedroom and ran her hand along the edge of the vanity. Behind her she could hear Aunt Dee saying, "Too much pattern. We need something solid."

Abolene knew her mother was different. None of her classmates had mothers that painted. Where other mothers might have pots of makeup and powder spread across their dresser, her momma had tiny tubes of paints and a cloudy glass of water with a thin bristled brush sticking out of it. An unfinished painting was spread across the veneer of the dresser.

The painting was of trees leafed out against the periwinkle blue of a dawning sky. Abolene had watched her mother lay down the background color. She had watched her mix and splotch color onto the crinkly paper until Abolene swore that she could see a light inside of it. Abolene swore that it was just like the sun was coming up inside of that paper. When the paint was dry her mother sketched winter trees across the face of the blue and then she died.

Julia had loved blue. She used to joke with Joe Skinner that she must love him because he was so black, he was almost blue. Joe would say, "I don't care why you love me. Just love me." Then he would wrap her up in his arms and kiss the living daylights out of her.

Abolene loved to watch this. She loved to watch her momma trying to struggle free, laughing and swatting Joe on the arm and saying, "Later for you, Bud." She meant later, when Abolene was not watching. She meant later, when Joe Skinner would lie down beside her mother in the four-poster bed and Abolene would lie in her own room, listening for murmuring and laughter and the rhythmic squeak of bed springs.

Behind her, Abolene could hear her aunts talking. They were considering the pink dress with the missing button again.

"I don't suppose it will show," Dee whispered.

Abolene touched her finger along the crinkled paper. It was rippled, like dry water.

Julia had liked to paint from photographs. For this unfinished painting of trees and the morning sky, she had gotten up early five days in a row and stumbled out into the yard wearing her nightgown and bathrobe and sneakers, carrying the Polaroid camera that Joe had given her. Julia had taken at least three pictures of every kind of tree there was in the front yard and these Polaroids were spread across the mirror of the dresser. Abolene squinted her eyes so that the patterns ran together.

"I suppose we could find another button," Dee was saying.

"It's the best one," Louisa replied. "With or without it."

Abolene turned around. "I want to keep these things," she said.

"The paints?" Dee asked. "Well sure, Honey. You ought to keep something of your mother's."

Beside the dresser there was a small wooden case that Julia had used to travel with her paints and Abolene leaned down to pick it up. When she did she saw the button, the pink button with the gold crimped edges, the one that belonged to the dress Aunt Dee was holding up, the dress her mother was going to be buried in. The button had rolled under the dresser and Abolene reached for it. When she turned around her mother's pink dress was lying across the bed, the arms spread wide as if to hug her.

18

When Abolene Redd packed her bags for the move to Chatham County, she folded up her grief the same as she folded her T-shirts and underwear and dresses and jeans. She layered it below her clothes and she layered it in the middle and she layered it on top. She smoothed her hands across it twice and clasped the suitcase shut.

There was no more room in that suitcase. That suitcase was heavy with grief and a young girl's clothes and Abolene carried the earrings home to China in one corner of her mother's paint box.

She sat in the window seat of a Greyhound bus and she rested one hand on its wooden top while the other hand fingered the wedding band on the string around her throat.

Abolene gazed out the window at the same farms and fields and houses that China had watched slip by when Earnest disappeared. The farms and the fields and the houses slipped behind her and Abolene turned her mother's wedding ring over in her fingers, spinning it on its string. Over and over and over again she turned it.

She had done this all through her mother's funeral, one hand on the wedding ring at her throat and the other jammed into the pocket of her dress, fingering the button she had found, the one that didn't show because the casket was closed to here.

Abolene had stood at the coffin and seen her mother lying there, surrounded by white satin and wearing the pink dress with the missing button. Only Dee and Louisa and Abolene knew that the button was missing. Only Abolene knew where it was and she stood with her hand in her pocket, her fingers touching the gold crimped edges and the smooth pink plastic and she whispered, "Momma," and then she whispered it again.

She touched the button so much that her Aunt Dee noticed her fingers moving inside the cloth of her pocket, moving like there was something alive in there and she came up behind Abolene and put her arms around her and led her away.

It wasn't until the bus was pulling out of the station that Abolene untied the string at her throat. It was just beyond Joe's garage that Abolene was threading the string through the button with the gold crimped edges. It was at a traffic light that she was tying it around her neck again. Abolene wore her mother's wedding ring and button for the rest of her life.

When China and George picked Abolene up at the bus station, China recognized her immediately. China gave a little noise up from her throat when Abolene stepped off the bus. China lay one hand on George's arm when the spitting image of her boy Earnest stepped down into her life.

She wrapped her arms around Abolene and pulled her closer, then she pushed her back and held her away. She looked Abolene over, up and down and finally declared, "You look just like your daddy did. Just like him. Doesn't she look like Earnest?" China asked George.

George said, yes, she did. He was heaving Abolene's suitcase into the bed of his truck. He wiped his brow and asked, "What you got in here, child?"

They rode together in the front of George's pickup truck. Abolene sat in the middle, crammed between the two of them. She rode looking straight ahead and saying nothing. She rode between them just as she had ridden on the bus between homes, silently, with one hand on her mother's paint box and the other at the homemade necklace at her throat.

The landscape passing by was lush and green. Jungles of kudzu vines heavy with fat green leaves roped their way up tall pine trees. There were fields of cows bowing their heads towards the grass. There were gas stations with old men sitting outside and younger ones leaning into the open hoods of cars. There was a river with a flat plane of dark water above the rushing dam.

"That's the Haw River," China said. "That's where William Lars Redd drowned. We're almost home."

Abolene nodded. She could have guessed it was the Haw River. She could have guessed its wideness and its spread of rocks and its brackish water. She could have guessed its snakes and birds and deer. She could have guessed its course because it coursed through her. Abolene Redd had the stories of the Haw River running through her veins just like water.

It was the same way with Roseberry. Before they had even reached it Abolene said the word, "Roseberry."

Then China pointed and said, "There it is. That's Roseberry," she said. "We'll go there on Monday."

George turned the truck into the driveway across the road from the big yellow house. They bumped along a rutted hard-packed lane that ran between two fields of cows. The cows raised their heads when the truck turned in. They raised their heads and mooed and some of them walked along the fence line when Abolene Redd arrived.

The scent of the house hit Abolene the minute she stepped inside. It was nothing like the smell of her mother's perfume or her paints and brushes or the grease from the cars that Joe was so often scented with.

The smell of China's house was the smell of a million things mingled together. It was the smell of old wood and grease and kerosene from the lamps that China still burned on occasion, of dust and cobwebs and stuffing coming out of quilts and babies coming out of mothers, of mothballs and cedar chests and bacon frying and hands wiped on aprons. It was the smell of stories breathing their ancient breath, but in 1966 Abolene Redd could not have named any of this. She only knew that it was strange and different and that the air here was stale and hot and that she missed her mother more and more with each step she took into Chatham County.

China reached behind her and flipped a switch beside the door, bringing to life a bare bulb hanging on a black cord from the center of the ceiling of the first room, a room that Gramma China called a parlor.

The walls were yellowed and the corners were hung with cobwebs. The floor was sloped and there were places that had been patched with the tacked-down lids from tin cans. The furniture, a couch, a chair and a table with a lamp on it, were worn and dulled with scratches and dust.

Abolene followed China through the house, China flipping light switches as she went, bare bulbs throwing shadows in her wake. They had not spoken since passing Roseberry, but when China opened the door to a small bedroom and swept her hand inside she said, "This is your room," and then she asked, "You brought the earrings, didn't you?"

"Yes, ma'am," Abolene said.

China twisted her hands together in front of her.

"They'll have to go under the house, you know."

China

19

It had been thirteen years since the earrings had been hidden safely away in the crevice of the corner piling. China tried not to think about that number and the things she had heard about it. She tried not to think about the possibilities of bad luck. She tried not to think about the bad luck of Julia dying and how it had been that bad luck that brought Abolene and the earrings back to Chatham County.

China tried only to think of Earnest coming home and when Abolene asked how long it had been since the earrings were hidden, China answered, "A long, long time." And when Abolene asked how long it would be before her daddy came home, China answered, "Any day now, I expect. Any day now."

She was on her knees at the time. On her knees in the hard-packed soil of the yard behind her house, with half her body folded and tucked underneath the floorboards. China was tugging at the crumpled page from Lydia Redd's book, tugging it out of the crevice and dropping it on the ground at Abolene's feet. She inched her fingers further inside that crack in the rocks and plucked out the other pieces of paper, the two folded pieces with the words she had written. Abolene picked them up and read them out loud, her own name plus abalone.

"It was just something I did," China said.

"Because Momma wouldn't give you the earrings?" Abolene asked.

"Just because. Just to help Earnest come home. Every little bit helps," China added.

"Then they should go back," Abolene said. "They should go back so my daddy can come home."

She folded the scraps of paper into neat little triangles. She unwadded the picture of Jennis and Lula Anne and William and read the caption. She ran one long brown finger across the earrings hanging off of Lula Anne Redd. She ran one long brown finger across the faces of William and Jennis. Abolene folded the page neatly and set it on the ground beside the snuffbox.

The snuffbox was lying beside China's left foot and she picked it up and twisted the cap off. Abolene watched her grandmother poke inside, push the rotten cloth apart and dig her finger into the cotton and pull one earring out into the sunlight.

"They don't look natural to me," China said, dangling the earring in the air between them.

The afternoon sun glinted off the gold trim of the earring and shone a thin line of light against Abolene's face. China saw it, saw that light jumping across that child's face, saw it travel across her eyes and cheeks and mouth and then saw it travel down her body and across the ground. She quickly put the earring back inside the box.

"I didn't mean for that to happen," China said.

"For what to happen?" Abolene asked.

"That. For the sun to catch the earrings and mark you with the light the way they did."

"Am I marked?"

China clamped the lid back on the box. "They've been out too long," she said and she folded her body back under the house.

Abolene could hear the metal scraping against the rocks. She squatted down and watched and when China crawled out and straightened back up, Abolene held out the folded scraps of paper and said, "Here. Every little bit helps." She dropped them into China's hand. "Every little bit helps," she said again.

China did not want Abolene to know that she had crammed those words into the crevice of the corner piling only out of desperation, only because Julia Redd had been so stubborn about putting the earrings back where they belonged. China did not want to say to Abolene, "And look what happened." Meaning, maybe your daddy would be here if not for that. Meaning maybe your momma wouldn't be dead. Meaning maybe you'd have another brother or sister by now, if only the earrings had been in the right place all along.

China didn't want to say these things to Abolene and instead she folded her fingers around the scraps of paper and disappeared under the house one more time. When she came out she sat back on her heels and asked her grand-daughter, "Do you want me to show you where they are?"

Abolene nodded. She let China take her hand and lead it to the rocks of the corner piling and along the rough stones until she felt the cool smooth metal of the snuffbox and the three pieces of paper crammed there.

"Do you feel it?" China asked.

"Yes, I feel it."

"It's going to bring your daddy home," China said. "And you won't be an orphan anymore."

It was at that moment that they both began their waiting. China waited for her son and Abolene waited for her father. They waited for years. They sat on the porch and waited. They weeded China's azalea bed and waited. They worked at Roseberry and waited. They walked to the cemetery every Sunday morning and when they came home and China's house came into sight, they both searched for the figure of a man sitting on the porch, waiting for them.

China fixed a big breakfast every Sunday morning. She fixed it for Earnest. She fried a whole package of bacon, four strips at a time laid across the bottom of her cast-iron frying pan and then lifted and drained onto a brown paper bag. She scrambled a dozen eggs, six at a time, cracked into a bowl and whipped with a fork and stirred into the hot pan. She toasted six pieces of white bread and left the butter out on the table to soften.

China scooped all this food onto her best platter and left it in the oven on low heat. She left a big glass of milk in the refrigerator. She set a place at the table and fancy-folded the napkin into a triangle and then she penned a note to her boy.

"Earnest," it said. "Went to the cemetery. Abolene is with me. You've been gone a long time, so I figure you're hungry. There's breakfast in the oven and some milk in the icebox. Love, Momma."

China pinned this note to the door with a six-penny nail that she drove in herself.

There was another note to China's boy, one for Monday through Saturday, and it read this way: "Earnest, Working at Roseberry. Come to the back door. Love, Momma."

In the first weeks after Abolene's arrival, China would scurry home from their walks to the cemetery and she would open the door to her house and call out his name. She would go to the kitchen and check the oven to see if the food was still there. China would pull the platter out and set it on the counter and silently count the bacon strips to see if even one was gone.

In the first few weeks after Abolene's arrival, China would pull the note off the door and ball it up and throw it away, only to write a new one the next morning. After a while China started rotating the notes, keeping Sunday's note to Earnest on the nail beneath the other one during the week, switching them back before they left for their walks to Cally's grave.

On Abolene Redd's first morning in Chatham County, China wrote out her first note to Earnest and she fixed him a big breakfast and left it in the oven.

"Where are we going?" Abolene asked.

"Visiting," China answered. "We got visiting to do."

They waited for the white Redds to leave for church, China sitting in the old recliner and Abolene on the top step leaning against the newel post.

"Why do we have to wait?" Abolene asked. "Do they mind you crossing their yard?"

"You'll meet them soon enough," China answered.

When they heard the car doors slamming and saw the blue Buick sliding out onto the highway, they rose up from their places on the porch. They walked down the lane between the fields of cows. They crossed the highway and stepped into the driveway of Roseberry. They passed the big house, the dining-room window with Mamie's wisteria planted outside and the back porch where the key was kept. They passed the rose garden and crossed the field with the tall, sharp grass slashing at their ankles. They stopped at one of the piles of rocks. They stopped at the logs that had once been cabins and China told Abolene about watching Riley tear them down on the day that Coyle was born.

"This one was Cally's," China said, holding one hand on the split-log step of the third cabin on the right. "Your daddy was started here with a man named Amzie."

"Started?" Abolene asked. "What do you mean, started?"

"It means this place is inside of us," China answered. "You and me and the children you're going to have. We'll never be rid of it."

Abolene picked up a stick and poked at the ruins of Cally's cabin.

"The earrings were here?" she asked.

"Cleavis lived here with Tom and Cally. Cally changed the color of her eyes right here inside this cabin." China leaned over and picked a tick off Abolene's leg. She tossed it on the ground. "I've felt Tom's sigh," China said. "He heaves it up from time to time and Roseberry gets cold in the middle of the summer. You'll feel it. Come on, now."

China held her hand out and Abolene took it and they walked along together, Abolene swinging the stick that she had picked up against the tall grasses. China felt her granddaughter's thin fingers in hers, the fingers of a child, so trusting and small, so like the fingers of Earnest. Maybe he would be home when they got back. It was the thought of Earnest coming home that made China scurry up the hill towards the two graveyards.

She only let Abolene stop twice, once to lean over the bridge and look into the mud-brown waters of the Haw River and again to roam through the white Redds' cemetery.

China sat on the stone bench while her granddaughter walked between the rows and read the stones.

Abolene pointed to a marble lamb and said, "Here's William." China took in a deep breath and smelled the sun baking on the boxwoods. China tried not to think about the sun that had glinted off the earring into Abolene's eyes. It didn't mean anything, she told herself. And neither did the number thirteen.

"Come on now," China finally said. "There's more important places to be."

Abolene followed her out of the iron gate. She ran her stick along the metal bars and listened to the latch click into place as China shut it. They crossed the bed of gravel that had been spread as parking for Riley Redd's funeral and they followed a small pine-needled path and stepped into the clearing of rocks.

"When the leaves are down," China said, "you can see the white Redds' cemetery from here. I hate that," she added. "I pure hate that.

"This one's Cally's," China said, laying her hand on one of the rocks. "This one's Tom's. This one's Tuly's."

"Who are the other ones?"

"We don't know."

20

China taught Abolene all that she could about Roseberry. She passed down all the stories that she knew, along with the secrets to polishing with lemon oil. She taught Abolene the names of the white Redds' portraits hanging on the staircase wall and she taught her how to fold and iron Lydia's white linen napkins into neatly creased triangles. She showed Abolene where Mrs. Redd kept her flask of vodka hidden in the drawer of her dresser among her bottles of jet-black hair dye and she showed Abolene how to thoroughly cut the shortening into the flour when making biscuits. China Redd taught Abolene all that she could about Roseberry and she hated doing it.

She hated shaking the child awake in the early morning hours before light. She hated nudging her into getting dressed and watching her sleepily follow China and her flashlight beam towards a day called work. China Redd hated most of all to see her own son's daughter slip the key from its hiding place on top of the light fixture and slide it into the lock on the back door of Roseberry.

That key unlocked so many things besides the door to the kitchen. In 1926 it had unlocked a lifetime of cooking and cleaning and "yes, ma'ams" and "no, ma'ams" for China. In 1966 it unlocked a summer's worth for Abolene, and China prayed that it was only a summer's worth.

China prayed that her grandchild would not spend her life brewing good pots of coffee and filling the creamer and getting the wet clumps out of the sugar bowl before breakfast. China prayed that her grandchild would not spend her life fanning away the hot, humid summers of Chatham County, waking and sleeping in China's rickety old house across the road from Roseberry, dusting the white Redds' portraits and cooking the meals and polishing the same silver that she had polished. It was the same silver that China had polished and China's mother, Earnestine, before her and before her, Abe's wife, Maude, and before her Cally working in the fields and touching dirt and rocks and never silver.

China Redd prayed that her boy would come home soon, come home and even though it meant leaving again, even though it meant leaving her behind, take the child away from here. Take Abolene where she can learn something beside these old stories and how to test the heat of an iron with a spit-licked finger.

China couldn't stand the thought of one more generation of black Redds working for one more generation of white ones. Already Lydia Redd had made comment over her good fortune at Abolene's arrival, over having such an able-bodied replacement for China. Lydia Redd had made comment on her good fortune but she never stuck a little extra pay in China's envelope for Abolene's help, and China was a little glad of that. It was better not to pay the child for work such as this. It was better to make her want to seek work somewhere else.

On the day that Lydia Redd made that comment, China grumbled to herself while washing the breakfast dishes with Abolene right beside her. "Don't own us anymore," China mumbled. "They don't own us anymore."

Abolene did not seem to notice. She walked alongside China in the mornings and the evenings. She worked alongside her in the days. She knew already when to say "yes, ma'am" and "no, ma'am" and when to say nothing at all.

She followed China every Sunday to the graveyard up on the hill and every Sunday she asked her grandmother, "Do you think my daddy might come home today?"

China answered that she hoped so. Or she answered that he might. Or she answered that it seemed likely, but as the summer wore on, going from one hot month into the next, even China started losing hope. But she never told Abolene that.

She never told Abolene that as day after hot day passed by, even she was starting to wonder if the earrings had been gone too long to have any power left. Even she was starting to wonder if Earnest would ever come home to claim his child and kiss his mother. Even China was starting to wonder if the dead man the police had found eleven years ago might not have been her son after all.

China thought about the coins and the key and the watch and the wedding band dropped into the crevice of the corner piling. China thought about the way that they had clinked against the rocks and the way that they were dropped down so far that they could never be retrieved again. China Redd remembered the sounds of them falling and she wondered if these were things that might have once jingled in the pockets of her boy's trousers.

But then China would tell herself that the key had not fit Julia's door. China would tell herself that it wasn't his key. It wasn't his wedding band. Those were not his coins. He couldn't have afforded a watch like that.

China would tell herself that the earrings were going to bring him home now. China believed it because it was all she had to believe and every morning while Abolene was getting dressed, China would carry her flashlight out into the yard and shine it under the house and into the corner piling. She would drop to her knees and tap her finger-nails against the snuffbox crammed between the rocks.

When she came back inside Abolene would be standing at the back door, twisting the wedding ring and the button that always hung from her neck and she would ask, "Are they still there?"

China would nod. "Still there," she would say. "Maybe today."

The summer passed. A calendar full of "maybe todays." A calendar full of "maybe todays" and shelling peas and cooking and scrubbing and sweeping and polishing and China telling Abolene everything she knew, telling it all in spite of herself.

China would point out the window above the sink at Roseberry. She would point to the rose garden and say, "That's where the kitchen house used to be. Maude cooked in it. It was John Redd that tore it down."

She would stand at the window of Coyle's room and point to a patch of weeds growing beneath a tree in the field.

"There's the pile of rocks that killed Riley," China would say. "Put there by the field hands. Some of them by Cally and Tom. It was their rocks that finally killed Riley Redd. They're running out of money, you know."

China would take Abolene downstairs and open the drawer to the secretary in the parlor. She would show Abolene the bills that were stamped with faint red "Past Due" notices. She would show Abolene the cracks in the plaster above the sideboard in the dining room. She would show Abolene the paint that was peeling off the sides of the house and falling in flakes among Mamie's wisteria and the azaleas out front. She would show Abolene the threadbare upholstery on the chairs in the parlor. She would point to the drip in the faucet upstairs and she would tell Abolene, "The white Redds are running out of money. They don't keep up with anything anymore."

China took Abolene to the attic one day. She lay the palms of both hands inside the bowl of a stair tread and told her whose feet had caused such a thing and then their own feet stepped inside those cups of wood and China turned around and said to Abolene, "It's a haunted life."

They climbed the stairs then, followed the same narrow staircase that the house servants had followed, cupped their toes into the wood of stair treads cupped and bowled themselves.

China showed Abolene the rows of wedding dresses, the boxes of papers, the trunks and dressers of ancient clothes. China showed Abolene soft leather gloves gone stiff with age. Boots with rotted laces and missing buttons. Hats with edges that crumbled at the touch of a finger.

China reached behind the old steamer trunk that sat below the strip of soot along the ceiling. China pulled out the oval picture of Bessie Redd and told Abolene that she was the woman who had shamed the white Redds by marrying a Yankee.

"They took her out of the Bible," China said and she opened the cracked leather Bible to show Abolene the page with Bessie's name crossed out with thick, heavy lines of black ink.

"Look here," China said.

But Abolene had wandered towards the vent. She was peering through the slats and stripes of shadow and sunlight lay across her face. She was peering through the slats at China's house across the road.

"Do you think he's coming home today?" Abolene asked.

Abolene

21

Abolene spent that first summer waiting and working. She followed China to Roseberry every day and she followed her home every night. She walked up the staircase past the staring eyes of the white Redds' portraits and she made the beds of the ones still living. She checked the oven when China made biscuits and she checked China's porch to see if Earnest was home. She fingered her mother's button and wedding ring hanging off the string at her neck and she silently waited.

It was the end of that first Chatham County summer when Abolene finally said to China, "Daddy isn't coming home, is he?"

"Of course he is," China replied.

They had just returned from the graveyard and the note to Earnest still fluttered on the door. The scrambled eggs and bacon and toast sat untouched, congealing and glazing over in the oven. The place setting sat neatly on the table. The napkin sat waiting for a lap.

Abolene noticed that China no longer called his name when she stepped inside the house. Abolene noticed that China had stopped anxiously looking when they crossed the backyard of Roseberry and her own front porch came into view. Abolene noticed that China no longer carried her flashlight to the back of the house in the mornings and Abolene had taken to checking on the safety of the earrings herself.

She had taken to dropping onto her knees in the same Chatham County dirt that Cally had knelt in. It was Abolene now who reached under the house and pulled the snuffbox out and twisted the cap off, who poked into Cally's cloth and field cotton and pulled one earring out and dangled it in the air. Sometimes the sun glinted off the gold trim and shined into Abolene's eyes, just as it had on the day that she arrived.

Abolene thought about China saying she was marked by that reflection. What had she meant by that? she wondered.

When she asked her, China replied, "We're all marked. All of us who are in this family are marked by those earrings," China said. Abolene thought that this must be true. In Chatham County there didn't seem to be any getting away from the past.

She remembered the day that her mother had given her the earrings, the day she had unexpectedly come into her room and handed her the rusty old snuffbox.

"They're earrings," Julia had told her, "and you're named for them."

Julia told Abolene the entire story that Earnest had passed along. She told her about William Lars Redd saying that the shell was called abolene and how that was the wrong word. She told her how Cally had changed the color of her eyes and stolen the earrings and how the white boy had drowned in the river after that. She told her about Maude hiding them after her baby died. She told her about China being born on the kitchen floor. She told her about Earnest stealing them and giving them to her in courtship.

"And then you were born," Julia said, "and we named you Abolene. I thought it was pretty."

"I'm named for a mistake?" Abolene asked.

"No, Honey. You're named for a story." Then she added, "Your gramma thinks they need to go back under the house."

"Why?" Abolene asked.

"To bring your daddy back."

"If you think it would help," Abolene said, handing the snuffbox back to her mother.

"It won't," Julia said, pushing it away with the palm of her hand. "It won't."

That was when Julia slid the gold ring off her finger and handed it to Abolene. By that time Julia Redd had come to believe that Earnest was gone forever.

She had come to believe that the dead man found in the wooded lot must have been her husband after all. The man whose key had not fit her door and whose wedding ring seemed a little too large for his thin, elegant fingers and whose coins had jangled and rolled and clinked against the watch in the bottom of a brown manila envelope. By that time Julia Redd had come to believe that the keys that Earnest had carried never really fit into the places that they needed to. By that time Julia Redd had come to believe that it was always she who had flung the doors of her own heart open. By that time Julia Redd was lonely.

Julia Redd needed company, company besides the child named Abolene, the child she had birthed and loved and raised alone. Julia Redd needed company besides the child who looked just like the husband she used to have. She needed the company of a man.

On the day that her mother gave her the wedding band and the earrings, Abolene twisted the cap off the snuffbox and took the earrings out to play with.

She wiggled the clasps and tried to break them open from the freeze of rust that covered them. She balanced them on the blonde nylon hair of her new doll. She tied a string around them and hung them from her own ears that way and looked in the mirror at their colors dangling against her almond-colored skin.

Then she put them back into the snuffbox. She nestled them into the rotten cloth that had once been something called a head rag. She rested them into the rough piece of cotton that was something called field. Abolene tucked the snuffbox into the drawer of her dresser. She buried it beneath T-shirts and underwear and she went into the kitchen and asked her mother, "Momma, what's a head rag?"

They went to the library that afternoon and Julia checked out a picture book on the Civil War. She carried it outside and they sat together on a hard, stone bench and Julia rested the book on her knees and opened it. She showed Abolene grainy pictures of black men and women standing in fields with hoes in their hands. She showed Abolene the cloth tied around the women's heads.

The shadows of sunlight shining through trees played

against the pages of that book and Julia said, "That's a head rag. Anyway, it's all over now."

"What's over?" Abolene wanted to know.

"Slavery."

"You mean us?" Abolene asked.

Julia turned the page to another picture, a picture of a big house, a house as large and tall as the house that Abolene would end up working in.

"That's a plantation house," Julia said. "It's a white people's house. Your father's people come from folks that worked a place such as that. Your Gramma China still works in that old house."

"What people do we come from?" Abolene asked.

"I don't know what people I come from," her mother answered. "But you come from me and your daddy. His people are your people too."

"Are they your people?"

"No," Julia answered. "Your daddy's people are not my people."

Julia closed the book and stood up. Abolene followed her back into the library. She watched her mother slide the book across the desk and say, "I'd like to return this please."

"Aren't we going to keep it longer?" Abolene asked.

"I don't want that book inside my house," her mother answered.

That book, that book with its pictures of big houses and fields and head rags and dead soldiers had been checked out for only twenty minutes. The same librarian took it back who had checked it out and she cocked her head at Julia.

Julia reached down for her daughter's hand. She held her head especially high and marched out of the library. She marched away from that history as best she could.

Roseberry was the kind of house that was in that book, and Abolene Redd went to work in Roseberry. She woke in the mornings with China. She got dressed. She held her grandmother's hand as they followed the bobbing flashlight beam towards the back porch light of Roseberry. She unwound the key's string from the light fixture and opened the back door.

Sometimes she heard China muttering, "It's not supposed to be this way."

Sometimes she heard China saying her prayers at night, "Please Lord, get Miss Abolene out of here. Not again, Lord. Not again."

Abolene Redd started drinking coffee two weeks after she arrived in Chatham County. By the end of that first summer she was drinking it without sugar. By the end of the next summer she was taking it black, letting the bitter hot liquid slide down her young throat, waiting for the jolt of awakeness that she knew it would deliver.

Every year on her birthday, Abolene Redd replaced the fraying string of her homemade necklace and said to China, "Daddy's not coming home, is he?" Every year on her birthday Abolene Redd went to the dogwood tree that grew at the corner of the house and felt its swollen buds and thought about her momma.

Whenever Abolene asked about her daddy coming home, China answered, "He has to. He has to come home. I'm an old lady now and he has to come home."

This was China's answer, even though she had stopped fixing Sunday morning breakfasts for Earnest and even though she never switched the notes on the door anymore. This was China's answer, even though she had stopped propping her boy's picture on the windowsill at Roseberry while she washed the dishes.

China was fifty-six years old now and forty-two of those years had been spent working inside that house. China's bones ached in the mornings and her back ached all day long. China's joints were stiff and creaking. The veins in her legs bulged under her skin. Her fingers were bent and uncooperative. She was moving slower and slower every day until finally Lydia Redd said to her, "Perhaps it's time for me to officially hire Abolene."

"She's in school," China said.

"Well," Lydia replied, letting her words trail off.

China knew what it was that Lydia Redd was not saying. China knew what was meant by, "Well."

Lydia Redd meant, well, let her quit. Lydia Redd meant, well, it's a waste of time for her to be studying. What would she do with the education anyway? And besides, she could be here, earning money.

"How old are you now?" Lydia asked China.

China didn't answer.

"Abolene's only fourteen," she said. "She's still in school."

"Well," Lydia said again. "She's a strong girl. I'm sure the boys are swarming after her like flies."

"She's in school."

China turned away from Lydia and plunged her hands

into the soapy water in the sink. The water was cold. It was early afternoon and China had let the breakfast dishes soak too long. China had rested in the sun on the back porch while Lydia had driven into town. China just didn't get things done the way she used to.

"She's a strong girl," Lydia said.

China heard Mrs. Redd's high heels clip across the linoleum floor. She heard the dining-room door swinging on its hinges. She looked out the window into the rose garden and started crying.

It was one month later, on a Thursday, that Martin Luther King Jr. was killed. Abolene had come to Roseberry after school, as she usually did. She sat at the enamel-topped table and studied her lessons as China busied herself with getting dinner ready. It was a Friday and it happened in Memphis and China and Abolene did not hear the news until they got home and turned on the radio in their own kitchen.

China did not know as she basted the ham in Roseberry that a shot had rung out in Memphis. Abolene did not know as she closed her schoolbooks and then piled China's hot biscuits into a cloth-lined basket that a man had fallen dead on the hard cement floor of a motel balcony. They did not know as they dished up peas and corn that eyes had fluttered and closed forever.

From the parlor China heard the low murmur of the television and then she heard it snapped off. She heard Lydia say something to Coyle. She clanked the oven door shut and did not bother to listen.

China and Abolene did not hear the news, although

surely Lydia Redd had. Surely Coyle Redd had. Surely they both knew as they sat in the dining room with their napkins laid neatly across their laps, as China and Abolene pushed through the swinging door, carrying to the table plates and bowls of steaming food. Surely they both knew as Abolene poured ice water and tea, as China poured coffee and set the creamer and the sugar bowl within reach.

Surely Lydia and Coyle Redd knew as China and Abolene Redd bagged up leftovers and cleaned the dishes and measured the coffee for the next morning, as Lydia Redd handed China her pay envelope early and said, "Why don't you take the next few days off, China? Both of you. You've been working mighty hard."

They walked home, puzzled, China feeling the pay envelope in her pocket and thinking it was a little fatter than usual. They walked home without talking, each of them wondering about it, each of them knowing that the other wondered about it too. They walked home and stepped onto the porch and then into the house that Joe and Alfie had built.

There were leftovers for dinner and Abolene dished them out onto two plates while China sat at the table and opened the envelope. There was another envelope inside with Abolene's name on it and China slid it across the table towards her granddaughter.

Abolene opened it and read the note inside.

"Abolene, I am sorry I have not been able to pay you until now. I appreciate all your help. Mrs. Riley Redd." It was ten dollars.

Abolene slid the money back to China. "You may as well keep it," she said. "Put it towards the household."

"There's something funny going on," China said.

Abolene set the plates down on the table. Outside a whippoorwill called at the edge of the woods.

"Do you want to listen to the radio?" she asked.

China nodded. They rarely listened to the radio. Its scratchy reception hardly made it worthwhile, but on April 4, 1968, China nodded yes to the radio and Abolene turned the dial and they sat down to eat.

"It doesn't surprise me," China said, when they heard the news. "This day has been too strangely quiet."

"It didn't happen till evening," Abolene reminded her.

"It doesn't matter," China said. "A day knows what's going to happen."

Friday and Saturday were strangely quiet too. Abolene and China weeded the few flower beds around the house and sat on the porch playing cards and listening for sounds of life coming from Roseberry. But there were none. Lydia and Coyle Redd stayed inside for two days but they went to church on Sunday.

Up in the graveyard, China and Abolene leaned up against Cally's rock and listened to the white people's church-singing drifting up the hill. They cleared the graves of sticks and stones and Abolene swept the ground clear. They walked back down the hill and picked enough wildflowers from the field beside the cabins to carry back up and place a spray on every single rock.

On Monday China returned to work. She walked down the lane in the dark. She unwound the key from the light fixture and stepped into the kitchen with its spread of gray linoleum floor. She made coffee and toasted bread and scrambled eggs. She stood at the kitchen window while washing the breakfast dishes and gazed at the sun speckling across the rose garden.

"Where is Tom's sigh?" China wondered out loud. "Why is the weather so nice?"

Coyle

22

It was a year later that Lydia Redd passed on and left Roseberry to its only heir.

It was time, the town's people said. She was a great lady, they said. The great lady of Roseberry. She went peacefully in her sleep, they assured Coyle, but they had no way of knowing.

And neither Coyle nor China nor Abolene would ever reveal the pile of sleeping pills on the nightstand, the bottle rolled under the bed and the cap nowhere to be seen and lodged somewhere in Lydia Redd's throat.

On the night that she died, Lydia Redd had reached for a handful of the blue capsules in the dark. She had opened the bottle and dumped them out onto the nightstand. She had reached for a handful of blue pills but instead had grabbed the cap and swallowed and caught it hard inside her windpipe. By morning the milky white skin of Lydia Redd had turned the same shade of pale blue as the capsules she took. By morning she was dead and it was China who found her.

Lydia Redd was buried next to Riley and the blank space of the double tombstone was filled with the usual information. The words, "Mother, Wife, Historian," were added. Hard stone roses were etched around her name.

Three days after she was in the ground, Coyle climbed the hill to the cemetery and creaked the gate open and lay himself down on the grass next to her. He reached his hand across and ran it through the raw dirt of his mother's grave. He looked at the sky and the trees, just tinged with the newness of spring.

Coyle Redd was lying in the exact spot where he would eventually be buried and this was not the first time that he had done so. This plot of ground had been waiting for him all his life and Coyle had lain himself down here many times. This was a plot of ground with Coyle Redd's name on it, a plot of ground with infinite patience.

His father had brought him here one day when he was very young. Riley had pointed to his own plot and then to Lydia's plot and then to Coyle's plot.

"Here," he said, drawing a box across the blades of grass with a stick. "Here," Riley said. "It's nice to know where you're going to end up, isn't it?"

The box that Riley drew was large, man-sized, and Coyle thought that it must have meant that his father expected him to live long enough to grow up.

Ever since that day, Coyle had spent time lying on the ground and checking his measurements against the imaginary line of his father's imaginary box. All his life Coyle had spent time in that cemetery, lying on the grass that would eventually cover him and running his fingers across the marble lambs of the children's tombstones.

If he grew up the way his father expected him to, he would never have a lamb to mark his place. It was only children who got marble lambs sleeping peacefully on their tombstones. It was only beloved children who got such lambs.

There was a story told to him about one of the graves with a marble lamb on top of it, told to him by both his father and China, but each one told it differently. It was a story about a baby named Lillian Ruth.

Lillian Ruth was the infant daughter of Lula Anne and Jennis, born in the woods and died in the woods. Lillian Ruth was born in the woods while Lula Anne hid along the banks of the Haw River, for fear of Sherman's troops marching in.

Coyle's father told him that Lula Anne was alone and that she was too weak to bury the dead baby and that she covered her with leaves and tried to mark the place to come back and get her.

China told Coyle that Lula Anne had been with the woman named Bessie, the one whose picture stayed hidden in the attic, the one whom Coyle had prayed to as a child.

China told Coyle that Bessie had bathed Lula Anne clean after she'd still-birthed beneath a tree in the woods. Bessie had bathed Lula Anne clean with a cloth ripped from her own skirts and dipped into the waters of the Haw River. She had soothed Lula Anne's fever and run her fingers through her sweat-drenched hair and when the time had come, she told Lula Anne that her baby was dead. It was Bessie who thought of the name "Lillian Ruth."

China told Coyle that Bessie dug a small hole, dug it with a stick and her own hands and she buried the baby there and muttered a prayer to God. China told Coyle that

Bessie hauled rocks from the bed of the Haw River and piled them on top of the grave so that it could be found again. China told Coyle that Bessie looked up at the tree, ran her fingers across the bumps that covered its bark and made note that it was a sugarberry. She looked hard at the river and made note of its curve and its width and the splay of rocks that it tumbled across and, if it didn't rise or fall too much, Bessie Redd was pretty sure that she could find the place again.

China told Coyle that Lula Anne and Bessie hid in the woods for three days and that was the same number that his father had said, although he'd never mentioned Bessie. China told Coyle that they were all home, Lula Anne and Bessie and Jennis, when Sherman's troops came marching up, and that was what his father had told him, minus Bessie, minus the troops.

It wasn't troops at all, China said. It was just a few men taking a trip into Chatham County and as far as they were concerned, the war was over and all they wanted from Roseberry was fresh water and to talk to a pretty girl, and they got both from Bessie Redd.

"Bessie climbed up on the horse of one of those soldiers and went for a ride," China said. "And when she came back home, Lula Anne and Jennis wouldn't even let her in the house. She didn't have any choice but to go off with that man. She was at his mercy then and that's why the grave of Lillian Ruth is an empty grave. She's buried out there in the woods somewhere. Only Bessie knew where."

Riley Redd had also said that Lillan Ruth's grave was empty, that when Jennis went into the woods and looked for the dead baby he couldn't find her, no matter how hard he looked. Riley Redd had told Coyle that a baby covered only with leaves like that probably attracted a wild animal. Riley Redd didn't finish but Coyle knew what he was saying. A wild animal came along and ate Lillian Ruth. But China said that the baby was buried, with rocks piled on top of her grave.

"How do you know all this?" Coyle had asked China.

"Because," China said, "when Jennis and Lula Anne refused to let Bessie back inside, she jumped up on that soldier's horse again and he steered down to the cabins and he rode between them and hollered, 'You're free now! You're free!'

"It was the first any of them ever heard of being free. And," China added, "Bessie yelled down to my great-granddaddy, 'Lula Anne's baby died,' she said. 'I buried her, Tom. I buried her beneath a sugarberry tree with rocks piled on top. You go find her, Tom.'"

"Why didn't he go find her?" Coyle asked.

China laughed. "Tom didn't have time to go find Lillian Ruth and Jennis never sent him."

Coyle was six years old when China told him this story. Her son, Earnest, was married and living in Raleigh and expecting a baby of his own any day now and China had been telling Coyle stories ever since Earnest had left.

She told him that her great-grandmother had changed the color of her eyes. She told him that there had been a child that got sold away. She told him that he was a boy, six years old, and they never saw him again.

"Imagine," China had said. "Taken away from your home at the very age you are now."

They had been sitting on the back porch, shelling beans when China told Coyle the story of Lillian Ruth. China ran her hand through the pan full of beans that sat between them and said, "That's enough."

She stood and put one hand on the small of her back and stretched the tension out. She looked out across the field behind the house, at the tree with the rocks below it, at the edge of the woods and the piles of logs and the opening trail that led to the cemeteries.

"Down in Georgia," China said, "you can still see the double chimneys of old plantations burned to the ground." China stretched. "Lillian Ruth is out there somewhere," she said.

Coyle Redd was twelve years old when he started looking for the dead baby in the woods. He spent a year roaming the banks and trails along the Haw River, looking for a sugarberry tree with a pile of rocks beneath it.

He was thirteen years old when he found a small heap of stones beneath the rotten stump of a tree. He couldn't say what kind of tree it was, but he sat down in the leaves beside it and looked at the bend in the river. He lay his hands on the rocks. He went back home and got a spade and shoved it into the ground beside the pile of gravestones and then he left it there.

He left the blade of the shovel jammed into the soft soil along the banks of the Haw River. He left it standing next to the small pile of rocks. He left it standing next to the rotten stump of a tree and that night, as he lay in the dirt in the yard beneath the pole lamp, as he heard China's singing over the rage of his father standing above him, as he gazed at his mother's black patent-leather shoes being dusted with dirt, Coyle Redd reached up and grabbed the belt out of the air.

23

Coyle Redd grew to the size of his father's imaginary box drawn across the grass in the cemetery on the hill. He grew up knowing that he was the sole heir to that small plot of land and the land below it and all that was left that could still be called Roseberry. He grew up knowing that there were cracks in the plaster and window frames rotting out and faucets that dripped loud and hard into the night. Even so, Coyle Redd could not have known how deeply in debt all that could still be called Roseberry was. Lydia Redd had hidden it well.

Coyle was twenty-one years old when his mother died. He was twenty-one years old when he inherited the cracked plaster and the shifting foundation and the rotten fascia boards of the big old house. He was twenty-one years old when he inherited the land and the weeds and the tumbled-down cabins and the pile of rocks that had killed his father. He was twenty-one years old when he inherited the secretary full of past-due bills but he had already inherited Riley Redd's yen for drink.

And he had already inherited his father's old insurance office in town. He had inherited the drive on weekday mornings along the highway to and from his office, the sound of the tires rushing across the pavement, the one traffic light at the one intersection. Coyle Redd had inherited a small, darkly paneled room and an old oak desk and a musty briefcase full of dormant accounts.

Coyle Redd had started this job two years before his mother died. For two years now he had been waking to the same alarm clock his father had awakened to. For two years now he had been getting out of bed in the mornings and showering and shaving. For two years now he had been putting on a suit and carrying a tie downstairs to drape across the back of his chair and knot around his neck, just before leaving.

Before his mother died Coyle had draped that tie across a chair in the kitchen, but after his mother died Coyle started taking all his meals in the dining room. This change was never announced. It just happened one morning. China found him there, sitting in his father's chair, waiting for his toast and coffee and spreading his newspaper across the gleaming mahogany top of the dining-room table.

Coyle Redd sat there just as Riley had done. He sipped his coffee and crunched his toast and snapped the pages of the newspaper in the air. Coyle listened to the snip, snip, snipping of George's pruning sheers as he cut back Mamie's wisteria.

George was the first one that Coyle let go. He couldn't afford him, but that was not what he told George. What he told George was that he needed the exercise and intended to do it himself.

Coyle patted his stomach and said, "It'll do me some good." He handed George his last pay envelope, shook his hand and said, "Good luck."

George walked away muttering to himself. "After twenty years," George muttered. "Twenty years I spent in this damn place and not even so much as a notice."

He tossed his shovel and rake and pruning sheers into the back of the truck. He dropped his pay envelope on the seat. He climbed into the driver's side. He turned the key and pedaled the gas and drove off, leaving a thick blue cloud of oil smoke in the air.

A light rain had fallen that day and a dry outline in the dirt marked where George's pruning sheers had lain next to Mamie's wisteria.

"You better dig up that wisteria vine," China told Coyle.

"I'll take care of it," Coyle answered.

China never knew what he meant by that. Was he going to take care of the wisteria by digging it up? Was he going to take care of it by keeping it pruned back? Was he going to take care of it by watering it and weeding around it and actually believing that it was a vine that would never grow and never die?

As it was, Coyle did nothing and it wasn't long before the vine proved that story wrong. Mamie's wisteria crept up the sides of the house. It wound its way under and along the boards of siding. It crawled towards the porch and twined its way up the newel post and crept its way across the roof.

China swore that Mamie's wisteria was stretching its wings for the first time in its life, finally feeling what it meant to be a wisteria vine. China swore that if someone didn't do something soon, that vine would smother all of Roseberry, house and land and barns and rocks.

"Just out of vengeance," China said. "If nothing else, that vine will take over just out of vengeance."

Mamie's wisteria was not the only thing that grew after George left Roseberry. The grass in the front and back yards grew thick and tall. The weeds choked out the flowerbeds. Moss grew up the sides of the front porch steps and honey-suckle climbed the newel posts and twined itself between the cracks in the floorboards. "You better get married and have you some young'uns," China told Coyle.

Coyle shrugged. There was no one he was interested in, although there were a few interested in him. The unmarried daughters of his mother's bridge club would present Coyle Redd with cookies and pies and unexpected company every now and then.

Even with Roseberry in such obvious decay, the unmarried daughters of his mother's bridge club persisted. They buzzed among themselves that all Coyle Redd needed was a good wife to straighten things out around there. They murmured that Coyle Redd must be grief-stricken over the death of his momma, to let things go the way he did. They agreed that the first thing any one of them would do if she was mistress of Roseberry would be to fire the old black woman and hire a younger one.

"The parlor's not dusted well," they said to each other. "The curtains need washing. Mrs. Redd would die to see it like that," they told their mothers.

The young women sat in the parlor of Roseberry, one at a time on Saturday mornings, and made polite conversation with Coyle. They told him, one at a time, about the pie they had just brought, about the recipe being handed down from their great-grandmother, about how they rolled out the crust themselves.

"With these very hands," they would say, holding up their hands in the air, white gloves shining into the darkness of the parlor.

They slyly tallied, one by one, the antique furnishings, the veins of cracks in the plaster walls, the displays of silver and china. They quietly wondered, each to herself, what it would take to repair that rip in the rug.

They crossed their legs so tightly that their knees shone white and Coyle Redd wondered what the point of such a woman would be. Besides, he didn't need them. He regularly visited a whore who lived further out of town, further down the highway, a woman named Vitra who lived in a tilting little shack up at the end of a long dirt road. Coyle paid Vitra cash money every Saturday night. He brought her money and trinkets and sometimes the pies that the other women had brought to him.

Whenever Coyle Redd came walking up the path to Vitra's house, carrying a pie, she would say, "Now I know you didn't bake that just for me."

Vitra would eat that pie with her fingers, licking each digit separately, slowly and deliberately and thoroughly.

Vitra would feed that pie to Coyle that way. It wasn't what the unmarried daughters of his mother's bridge club intended to happen to the pies that they baked themselves.

Coyle thought that it was worth every bit of money he paid. It was worth every bit of money he paid not to be sitting in the parlor with a white-gloved woman whose legs might never come uncrossed. It was worth every bit of money, even though there were bills being left unpaid.

Coyle Redd and Roseberry were sinking deeper and deeper into debt. The bills inside the secretary grew as high as the grass and the weeds outside.

Coyle Redd cashed his paychecks at the bank every Friday. He bought two bottles of liquor and three quarts of ginger ale. He set aside the money for Vitra, folding the bills and tucking them behind his driver's license inside his wallet. He counted out China's pay for the week and put it into an envelope and gave it to her every Monday morning.

Every Monday morning China found that envelope sitting on the kitchen counter next to the sink, weighted down with the sugar bowl. It was exactly how Lydia had paid her and Emma before her. China found that envelope every Monday morning until she finally stopped coming, or tried to.

She called Coyle on a Tuesday night and told him, "I'm too old now and it's only you. There's not much to do these days," China said.

The truth was that there was plenty to do, but China Redd didn't think that she could face it anymore. The truth was that the house smelled and China Redd could hardly stand it.

Roseberry smelled like Riley again. The same fermented scent of liquor that had been in Riley's skin was in Coyle's skin now. It was sour and rank and it permeated every piece of clothing that he wore. It permeated the towels China washed and the sheets she folded and the upholstery she vacuumed.

It permeated the air and China choked on its fumes. All day long, she kept the doors and windows of Roseberry flung wide open, no matter what the weather was. All day long she kept fans blowing. All day long she kept the slats in the attic vent turned to let the air in, but even fresh air couldn't help. Even Tom's sigh couldn't knock out this smell.

"How will I eat?" Coyle asked on the night that China called. "I don't even know where the coffee is."

China didn't say anything. She stayed on the line and let Coyle think about where the coffee might be. She stayed on the line and listened to him opening and closing the cabinets in Roseberry's kitchen. She let the dead silence accumulate between them.

"What about Abolene?" Coyle asked.

"She's only sixteen," China said. "She's still in school."

"I'll pay her," Coyle said.

"I'll work till you find someone," China offered. "But leave Abolene out of this."

China came for another week and then another and then another until a month had passed by without Coyle having replaced her. Every day China thought, maybe. Maybe today. China did not know it, but she would work at Roseberry until the end.

She was there the day that Coyle Redd unfolded a page torn from a magazine and spread it across the top of the dining-room table. It was an advertisement for a Winnebago, and it pictured the mammoth bus parked next to a river with mountains in the background. It pictured a white couple cuddled beside an open fire along the banks of the clear, running river. "Get Away," the advertisement said. China was pouring Coyle's morning coffee when he unfolded this piece of paper. She poured his coffee and leaned down to pick his tie up off the floor, where it had slid from the back of the chair.

Coyle spread the creases out of the page with the flat of his hand. He thumped his finger against the picture and said, "I'm selling everything, China. I'm selling Roseberry. I won't be needing Abolene. I'm having an auction."

China

24

China could not believe that what Coyle Redd meant was to sell it all, all of Roseberry and everything in it, but that was exactly what Coyle Redd had meant. He called three different auction companies to come look over his estate. To China's eyes they all seemed the same.

The auctioneers arrived on separate days, driving brand-new pickup trucks and wearing brand-new cowboy boots. Each one was tall and white and wore a hat with a wide, curled-up brim. When China answered the door, each one nodded and looked at a piece of paper in their hands and said, "Mr. Redd, please."

China would show each one into the parlor and then watch his eyes roaming around the room, taking a silent inventory of what a sale like this might bring.

Coyle would show the man around the house. China would hear them upstairs, walking through the bedrooms, opening drawers and closets and peering into boxes and trunks. She would hear them climbing the attic and shuffling around way up high in the house, one whole floor between her in the kitchen and them in the attic with the wedding dresses and the portrait of Bessie and the old cracked-leather Bible. China would hear the boxes being pushed across the floor. She would stand at the sink and watch them walk across the yard towards the barn. She would imagine the man resting the toe of one brand-new cowboy boot on the tire of the old blue tractor.

As far as China knew, only one of the auctioneers suggested to Coyle that he think about it. He said it while sitting at the kitchen table with a yellow legal pad spread in front of him.

"I've been thinking about it all my life," Coyle said.

The man slid his card across the enamel towards Coyle. "When you've made up your mind," the man said.

This was not the one that Coyle hired. Coyle hired the one who sat at the kitchen table and propped one boot on the chair in front of him and said to China, "Do you come with the place?"

"No sir," China said. "I sure don't."

"We could auction. . . ." The man began and then stopped. Coyle Redd had stepped back into the room.

China stood at the sink with her hands plunged into cold water, washing potatoes and listening to the scratch of the pen across the contract Coyle was signing. It was the first of July. They would start on Monday morning.

The man's name was Mr. Jackson, and he showed up on Monday morning with a crew of young boys and instructions from Coyle Redd to do the kitchen last and stay out of China's way.

They started in the attic. They climbed the bowled-out stair treads without a thought, making lists of everything they found. Mr. Jackson assigned a value to each item.

They assigned numbers to every piece of Roseberry, starting with the attic.

They tagged every single wedding dress and hat and veil and pair of gloves. They stuck yellow stickers on the inside door of the old Victrola. They stuck stickers onto dressers and trunks and wardrobes.

They boxed up sheaves of papers, papers nibbled by mice and thin and brittle with age. They boxed up old journals and bibles and letters and diaries. They even tagged the big family Bible, the one with the cracked-leather cover and the names and the birth dates recorded in it, the one with Bessie Redd's name crossed out with straight black lines of ink.

"Auction isn't even a pretty word," China told Abolene one afternoon, sitting in the kitchen of Roseberry.

Abolene nodded. They were both thinking the same thing. They were both thinking of Cleavis, sold to a slave trader, stood up on a block somewhere, bought by a stranger.

The auction was scheduled for August fifteenth.

"The Historical Roseberry Estate," the sign said.

"August 15," the sign said.

"Come early."

There were flyers for the auction all over town, flyers stapled to the posts of street lamps, flyers anchored under windshield wipers in parking lots, flyers stacked beside the cash registers of gas stations and grocery stores and folded into the pockets of patrons, dropped into brown paper bags on top of cereal and bananas.

The flyers could not list everything that was for sale,

could not list everything that China had ever cleaned, could not list the gallons of dishwashing liquid or oil soap or the pounds of silver polish used in China's lifetime on the things that people would buy and cart away and live with.

The lists did not say any of the things that China wanted to say. These lists were as empty as the cups of the stair treads leading to Roseberry's attic. Empty as a bowl but full of the things not said. Empty as air but full of things gone. The lists said nothing about the piles of rocks that still speckled the cleared fields surrounding Roseberry. The lists said nothing of the crumbled cabins at the edge of the woods. The lists said nothing about the empty scar of land beneath the rose garden. The lists said nothing at all, as far as China was concerned.

The auctioneers swarmed through the rooms of Roseberry every day like clouds of locusts. Every day one of the young boys would squeak the swinging door from the dining room open and step into the kitchen with something for China to clean.

Everything must be cleaned. Everything must be inventoried. Boxes were stacked and piled everywhere. Furniture was tagged and rugs were rolled, chairs were edged against the walls of the parlor and hallway, spaces were cleared and then filled, drawers were dumped and contents inventoried and tagged or boxed.

Even sets of sheets had yellow tags hanging off them. Even sets of towels. Even sets of clothes from Lydia's and Riley's closets.

The local unmarried girls stopped bringing pies and

cakes and cookies to Coyle on Saturdays. There was something terribly wrong, they thought, with a man who would sell his family's things. But even so, they buzzed with the rest of the town and county over the upcoming auction.

People all across Chatham County speculated about what they might buy. They looked at the pictures in Lydia Redd's book and pointed to pieces of furniture. They pointed to the pink fainting couch that William leaned against, to the shapely table that Mamie's hand rested on, to the chair that Jennis stood behind. They pointed to the furniture and said to each other, "I'm going to try and buy that."

China stayed in the kitchen where the auction company was not yet allowed. But that didn't stop them from bringing her silver to polish or bedspreads to launder or a stack of bowls to clean.

One stack of bowls had come from the barn. It had been stored in its wilting cardboard box at the back of an empty stall. The bowls were caked with dust and spider webs and wedged behind them was a wad of boys' shirts. The soft cotton madras shirts of a boy, with buttons missing and rips in the fabric and the stiff spread of dried blood across the back.

China knew that these were Coyle's old shirts, the shirts that Lydia had whisked away in the mornings after Riley had lost his temper. The shirts of a young boy who had made a homemade altar in the attic and of a somewhat older boy who had slept on China's porch one night and had lay his head in her lap the next day. These were Coyle's old shirts and China plunged them into the depths of a grocery bag and buried them beneath garbage of ham bones and carrot peelings and an empty baking-soda box.

Everything else, China cleaned. She would sit at the kitchen table with a bowl of soapy water and a rag and an old toothbrush and for the last time China would scrub the crevices of the cut-glass vase that Lydia's wedding flowers had come in. For the last time she would polish, until it shined like a silver headlight, the tea set that Mamie had used. For the last time China would soak and scrub the bowls that had been stacked and forgotten in the stalls of the barn.

China sat at the kitchen table of Roseberry and piece by piece cleaned her own history for a sale that would bring her no money. Piece by piece she felt the familiar objects pass through her hands. She felt the familiar curve of the silver gravy boat and the familiar cut of the crystal goblets. She felt the familiar crimped edges of ancient bowls, the fissures of cracks across plates never used anymore, the collars and cuffs of Riley's old shirts, the soft cashmere of Lydia's old sweaters. Everything got cleaned for the auction.

The very word "auction" caught in China's mind like a trapped bird. It fluttered there, the sound of its wings beating like a heart. It exhausted itself trying to escape. It fluttered and beat itself inside her mind, until it lost its feathers, until its eyes got wild, until it stayed still, lodged and caught, but not yet dead.

25

In the middle of July a representative from the University of North Carolina in Chapel Hill climbed the tall, steep steps to the porch of Roseberry and rasped his knuckles against the front door. He wanted to speak to Coyle. He wanted to ask him if he would make a donation, perhaps of historical papers, to their collection at the university.

Coyle refused. He complained about it to China. He came into the kitchen where she was sitting at the table polishing silver and he said, "How do they expect me to pay off my debts if I go giving everything away?" Coyle Redd threw his hands up in the air. "How the hell can I ever buy my Winnebago if I give things away? It's just like it always was," he said.

China told Abolene later that night that she knew what Coyle Redd had meant by that. It's just like it always was, he meant. We're taking care of everybody.

China had heard this before about the slaves who had cleared the fields and toted the water and cooked and cleaned and emptied slop jars. She had heard John and Emma talking to guests at a dinner party one night, a long time ago when she was young. John was talking about how things were in the old days, how the family had fed and clothed an entire community of thankless slaves. John was talking about how they had taken care of every-thing. "Everything," John Redd had said, as he took a drink off the tray that China offered. "Everything. And they all left. All except for Tom's family. Loyal to the core," John said. "Tom and his wife stayed on out of pure loyalty and love. China here's descended from them."

Walking home that night, China told her mother what John Redd had said. Earnestine draped her arm across her daughter's shoulders and spoke. "Your father's family stayed because of Cleavis."

"Cleavis is dead now," China said. "But we're still here."

"We got land now," Earnestine told her. "We got land and our very own house built by your daddy and his brother. And besides," she added, "where would we go?"

They had stepped up on the porch right as Earnestine said this and Joe opened the door and stepped outside. The soft light of a kerosene lamp shone behind him. China's father smiled.

"I bet you're tired," he said. He kissed Earnestine and then leaned down to kiss China. China was tall and Joe didn't have to lean down far. "I bet you're real, real tired," he added.

In the days before the auction, China started thinking about the earrings again. She thought about the house slave who must have stolen the earrings for Cally. She thought about his feet scurrying down the attic stairs to close the shutters on the night of Tom's bone-chilling sigh. She thought about the fact that the earrings would be a part of Coyle's estate if not for the man with the feed sack wrapped around his face.

As the date of the auction drew nearer, Coyle began avoiding China, as much as a man can avoid the woman who feeds him. He looked down as she served him. He looked away when she spoke to him. As the date of the auction drew nearer and nearer, Coyle Redd began spreading the creased picture of the Winnebago across his desk at work, across the dining-room table at meals, across the counter in the bathroom while he brushed his teeth. Coyle Redd began gazing at the picture of the Winnebago as though it was a picture of a lover, a picture of a person, a picture of a woman who might someday return to him or take him away.

China finally asked him, "Doesn't it bother you? Doesn't it bother you to sell everything that you grew up with?"

"No," Coyle answered, "it doesn't bother me at all." He snapped his paper in the air and pretended to read.

You'll be just as haunted, China thought. Roseberry won't go away. Just because you sell it doesn't mean it's gone.

"We all have our history," China said, topping off his coffee and sliding the last biscuit onto his plate and scooting the creamer and the sugar bowl closer to his reach.

It was the next day that Coyle Redd came into the kitchen with a sack of frozen dinners. China watched him file them one by one onto the frosty shelves of the freezer. She watched him turn around and duck his head. She watched him reach into his vest pocket and pull out a white envelope and hold it out in the air towards China.

"Two weeks' worth of pay," he said. "I won't need you anymore. They start the kitchen tomorrow."

China took the envelope from Coyle. She opened it

right in front of him and counted the bills, nodded and put it in her purse, clasping it shut with a final click.

"What will you do?" Coyle asked. He nudged his toe across the floor and looked down at the black mark he'd just made.

"I'll think of something," China answered, looking down at the same black mark across the shining gray linoleum.

China thought about the large white sign at the end of the driveway. It was left there, sitting on the flat, wooden trailer of a truck. Its plastic letters were eight inches tall and they spelled the unpretty word "Auction."

"Are you coming to the auction?" Coyle asked her. "It might be fun to bid on some stuff."

"There's nothing I want," China said.

"Look, China." Coyle loosened his tie and pulled it off through the collar of his shirt. He looked at China for the first time in weeks. "Look," he said again. "Look, it's our . . . it's your last day here and I was wondering . . . I was wondering if you could . . . if you would . . . have dinner with me . . . have dinner with me in the dining room?"

China let her eyes wander to the oven light, to the closed door where a plate of roasted chicken and creamed corn and rolls were keeping warm. She had cleaned that oven the day before. She had sprayed it with that awful-smelling foam. She had spread newspapers on the floor and gotten on her hands and knees and pulled the yellow rubber gloves up as far as they would go. That oven was clean. The burner rings shined. The top gleamed. There was no cake of grease built up behind the knobs or the clock or the timer. China could hear the clock in the silence that stood between her and Coyle Redd. China could hear the clock's rhythmic clicking, whiling away whatever time she had left inside of Roseberry, whiling away a few minutes' time the same as it had whiled away her life.

China looked down at the gray linoleum floor. She had scrubbed it and waxed it that very morning. Except for the one black mark made by Coyle in front of the refrigerator, the gray linoleum floor shined like a placid lake.

China looked at the sink of soapy water, at the greasy broiler pan soaking there, at the wadded dishrag on the counter, the yellow rubber gloves draped across the divider of the sink.

China looked through the open swinging door, into the dining room, at the one place setting that was laid on the table, the white linen napkin creased into a crisp triangle, the silver knife and fork and spoon beckoning his use, the water goblet, the iced tea glass, the cup and saucer waiting for coffee.

It was laid out like this every day, creamer and sugar bowl, trivets waiting for hot plates of food, serving spoons waiting, chairs waiting.

It was laid out like this every day, according to how many of the white Redds were still alive and eating. It was laid out like this every day and always had been for as long as China Redd could remember. The only difference was Mamie's wisteria growing thick across the window now. The only difference was the way the sunlight filtered through its leaves and splattered shadows across the mahogany table.

"No," China said. "I need to go home."

China did not serve Coyle the last meal she ever cooked there. China did not carry the platter of chicken and the bowl of corn and the basket of rolls to the table.

China just looked at him and said, "Your dinner's in the oven."

It was August seventh. The year was 1970. China Redd left Roseberry for the last time. China Redd picked her pocketbook up from the white enamel table. She looked once again at Coyle standing by the refrigerator with its store of frozen dinners.

"Good luck," she said.

She glanced once more around the kitchen at the floor, the pans, the dishes she had used every day for almost all of her life, the braided rug she had stood on in front of the sink. China turned away from the kitchen of Roseberry and twisted the doorknob open and stepped outside. She slipped the key from the pocket of her dress and looped its string onto the light fixture. She listened to her feet echoing down the steps. She listened to her feet pad across the grass. She listened to her feet crunch along the gravel of Roseberry's driveway.

China Redd left by the same trail that she had come in on. She left by the same lane that her mother had walked. She left at the whim and the need of a white man, the same as she had arrived. Her mother would have called it survival.

"It's just survival," Earnestine would have told her. "It's just survival. God never intended for this to happen."

Then why did it? China would always wonder. Why did it happen?

Leaving Roseberry early was the reason that China Redd got home before dark. It was the reason that she set her pocketbook with its pay envelope tucked inside on the top step of her porch and laid her flashlight beside it. It was the reason that China Redd walked around the edges of her own house and lay her hands against the siding, against the grimy panes of glass, against the chipped paint of the windowsills and the worn, spotted steps of the back stoop.

It's ours, China thought. This house is ours.

China Redd walked around the edges of the house three times, until finally she found herself at the corner of the kitchen where she dropped to her knees in the hard-packed dirt. It was the place where the earrings were kept. It was the place where she tucked her body under the house. It was the place where she felt along the rough rocks to the empty crevice in the corner piling. It was the day that everything changed.

Abolene

26

China did not know that Abolene had been wanting something pretty, but she should have known it. Every young girl wants something pretty. China herself had held the earrings to the sides of her neck the same as she had seen her mother do. China herself had wondered what it would be like to put them on.

China did not know that Abolene had been wanting something pretty and that one of the pretty things she wanted was a pair of earrings to show off the shine of almond-colored skin along her neck. Another one of the pretty things that Abolene wanted was a new dress that she had seen inside the pages of a J. C. Penney catalogue. Another one of the pretty things that Abolene wanted was a boy named Leon Jordan.

Leon Jordan had skin the color of a butternut squash. He had eyes as deep and black as pools of water in the bottom of twin wells. He had dark wavy hair that rode like chocolate icing across the top of his head. China would not have liked him.

China would have said that his name was too much a mixture of things, too much rhythm and blues at the beginning of it and too much church music at the end.

China would have said that his skin was too light and his eyes were too dark and his hair was too slick to be the hair of a boy headed into becoming an honest man. China would have said that Leon Jordan's fingers were too stubby to be entwined with the thin, elegant fingers of her grandchild. China would have said that the two of them didn't belong together and Leon Jordan would have said the same thing, until he saw Abolene Redd wearing a pair of antique seashell earrings.

It was on China's last day at Roseberry that Abolene stole the earrings. It was in the afternoon and a hot sun baked the fields and caused the highway to shimmer in the distance. Clouds of bugs rose out of scorched grasses like pieces of torn lace.

Things were dry and dusty when Abolene crawled under the house and pulled out the snuffbox and listened to the metal scraping against the rocks. The pieces of paper fell out with the earrings and Abolene left them lying on the ground.

Abolene Redd sat on the back steps of China's house with the snuffbox held between her legs and a can of WD-40 and an old dishrag next to her. She sprayed the earrings with oil, dousing each one down so much that it dripped and left spots on the worn, wooden steps. She wiggled the clasps back and forth and sprayed the earrings some more and wiggled them some more until finally the freeze of rust broke and Abolene Redd could open and close the earrings as easily as the day that they had lay in the palm of Cleavis's hand.

Abolene wiped the oil off with the dishrag. She rubbed

every swirl of color in the teardrop shapes. She rubbed the pitted gold trim until it shined. She wiped the clasps clean.

Abolene Redd carried the earrings into the bathroom and tried them on. She pulled the cord to the bare bulb that hung from the ceiling. It's light glared into the mirror as Abolene Redd turned her head this way and that. She looked at the pitted gold trim and the swirls of seashell colors against the colors of her own skin.

She hid the empty snuffbox on a ledge inside her closet. She slipped the earrings into her pocketbook along with half a roll of breath mints. Abolene Redd walked down the lane towards the hot, shimmering highway and then she walked the four miles into town.

A block away from the back of the Piggly Wiggly, where Leon Jordan would be hanging out with his beautiful skin and his group of friends, Abolene Redd slipped the earrings out of her pocketbook and onto the lobes of her ears. She slid a breath mint into her mouth and sucked hard as she walked. Abolene Redd walked right up to the butternut boy with the wavy hair and said, "Hi, Leon."

It seemed that Abolene Redd might do anything while wearing those earrings. It seemed that Leon Jordan might do anything too.

He opened the car door for her just like she was a lady. He took her for a drive to a field outside of town. He pressed his mouth into hers before she was ready. He pushed her down into the rough grass and pulled her skirt up.

Abolene felt the burning between her legs. She felt a rock lodged in the small of her back. She heard Leon

Jordan grunting on top of her and Abolene thought about what China had told her that her mother once said. "I never seen such a rocky place as Chatham County. It's downright unfriendly."

Leon Jordan drove her home. He dropped her off at the end of the lane leading to the little house across from Roseberry. He sped off in the night and burnt rubber across the highway. Abolene could see the porch light on. She could see China sitting in the old blue recliner. She could see China stand and look out towards the road.

It was the day that everything changed, the day that the last of the black Redds ever worked inside Roseberry, the day that the last of the white Redds ever took a breath.

It was the day that Abolene came home with her dress in disarray, with blades of grass and straw sticking from her hair, with a pain and a stickiness between her legs, left there by Leon Jordan.

It was the day that Abolene returned the earrings to China. She dropped them in China's open palm and said, "I'm sorry." It was the day that Abolene said, "These earrings ought to never see the light of day."

It was the day that a seed was planted inside of Abolene and started to grow into a baby, another generation, another child to be born on land that had once been Roseberry's land.

It was one hell of a day, China would say later. It was one hell of a day. It started with leaving Roseberry, with leaving Coyle's dinner in the oven, with refusing to sit at the table with him. Then there was the problem of the missing earrings, gone once again from the crevice of the corner piling. When China's fingers came up empty from the crevice, they fell to the gound and found the folded picture of Lula Anne and her family and one scrap of paper with the words, "Abalone earrings," written on it.

China searched Abolene's room, turned the clothes of Abolene's dresser out onto the bed and rifled through them. Ran her hands between the mattress and the box springs. Crawled on her knees to look under the bed. Fiercely scooted the clothes inside her closet across the metal rod.

That was where she found the snuffbox, but not the earrings. The snuffbox fell out of the closet and clattered at China's feet as it rolled across the floor. When China twisted the cap off, it was empty except for Cally's cloth and Cally's cotton and the air that China had come to think of as Tom's own breath.

China thought of the air inside the snuffbox as being the same air that had been trapped inside when Tom first gave the box to Cally. No matter how many times the snuffbox was opened, China thought of the air inside as Tom's breath, like his sigh that had circled Roseberry like wind one night, only this breath was trapped inside.

China waited for Abolene. She would wait all night if she had to. She turned on the porch light and sat in the recliner with the moths fluttering up above her. She sat with the snuffbox sitting in her lap. She sat with her fingers drumming across its closed metal lid. China waited for this reckless child named Abolene to come home. Just like her daddy, China thought. Abolene Redd is just like Earnest used to be.

When China saw the headlights of Leon Jordan's car slow down along the highway, she sat up straight. She watched Abolene stiffly get out of the car and take a few taut steps. She watched the car speed away and she smelled the stench of Leon Jordan wasting his tires along the asphalt in front of Roseberry.

China labored her way out of the too-soft recliner. She leaned against the newel post and watched Abolene in the moonlight, walking slowly towards the house. China could hear her feet on the ground, shuffling like an old woman's feet against the hard-packed soil. China watched her granddaughter stumble in ruts that she should have known were there.

China made her way off the porch and stood in the yard. She set the snuffbox down on the top step. She waited and watched as Abolene walked slower and slower with each step, until finally China went out to meet her and wrapped her arms around her said, "What happened?"

"Here," Abolene said. She reached up and pulled the earrings off and handed them to China. "Here," she said. "They don't belong to me. They don't belong to anyone."

China wrapped her fingers around the teardrops of shell and gold trim, polished to a shine by Abolene's rag and the can of WD-40, polished to a shine by the oil from Abolene's skin, polished to a shine by Abolene's fingers working them like beads inside her pocket as she had walked to town. China opened and closed the clasps.

Abolene pulled her skirt straight. She lay one hand across her cheek and looked at China and China could see the moistness in her eyes.

"What did he do to you?" China asked.

Abolene picked a blade of grass out of her hair and felt the cut in her back where a rock had lodged itself as she lay on the hard ground of a field down a dirt road somewhere in Chatham County. Abolene thought about the grunts of the butternut boy on top of her. She thought about him rolling off her and looking up at the sky.

"I don't know what you're crying about," Leon Jordan had said. He stood up and pulled his pants back to his waist. "You got to grow up sometime."

"I didn't want that to happen," Abolene choked.

"You're crazy. You told me yes. Do you want a ride home or not?" he asked.

Leon Jordan zipped his pants and began buttoning his shirt. Leon Jordan turned away and walked towards the car. Abolene lay there. She heard the door slam and the engine start up. She heard him pedaling the gas like a question mark. Are you coming?

When he dropped her off at the end of the driveway, Abolene turned to him and said, "I don't ever want to see you again."

He laughed. "I was going to say the same thing to you," he said. "The exact same thing."

"Did he rape you?" China asked, as she stood in the yard, stood looking at her granddaughter's ruffled clothes, looking at the rip of fabric across her shoulder, looking at the smear of dirt across her cheek, feeling the antique earrings burning heat into the palm of her hand. "Did he rape you?" China asked again.

"No," Abolene said. "It was my fault."

China watched her climb the steps, holding her hand against her back like an old woman. She watched the creak in her walk, the way she wobbled at the door, the way she steadied herself with one hand held against the back of the recliner. China watched the moths fly around Abolene's head and slip inside the house with her.

She looked up at the sky, at the faint light of the moon, at the bright beauty of the North Star. China knew that it had guided people away from plantations like Roseberry. It had guided people to a place where folks with skin the color of hers or lighter, or darker, could be free.

Her father had pointed it out to her one night. He had carried her out into the yard propped on his hip and pointed to that bright, bright star. "They used to follow that star," Joe told his only child. "We're still trying to follow that star."

From inside the house, China could hear Abolene running bath water. She could hear the creak of the floorboards.

She thought about her uncle Alfie sliding off the roof and crumpling onto the ground. He landed right here, China thought, looking down at her shoes. He built us a house and then landed right here.

China picked up the snuffbox from the top step of the porch and twisted the lid open. She made the bed for the earrings with her fingers and dropped them in and clamped it shut. When she turned around she saw Roseberry like she always had, looming against her own horizon like it always had.

The back porch light was left on as though she would

be coming to work tomorrow. The lights in the windows were muted by the closed curtains. There was a tiny orange glow, coming and going on the front porch and China knew that Coyle was sitting there in the dark, smoking a cigarette. She had seen the same glow from Riley's cigarettes and John's cigars. China could hear the squeaking chains of the porch swing as Coyle Redd kicked it into motion.

China sighed. She wished for a sigh that was as big and cold as Tom's sigh had been. She wished for a sigh that could change things. She wished for a sigh that could take this night away, but China Redd was tired and there was no such sigh inside of her. China Redd was tired and she hid the earrings back where they belonged. She tucked the picture of Lula Anne and Jennis and William back into the crevice. She tucked beside it the piece of paper with the words "Abalone earrings." China stood and dusted the Chatham County dirt from her knees.

She went inside and knocked on the bathroom door.

"Did he rape you?" China asked again.

"No," Abolene said. "It was my fault. I told you."

"Are you sure?" China asked.

Abolene splashed water on her face. She could feel that her muscles were irked. She could feel a stiffness up inside of her that had not gone away with Leon Jordan. She closed her eyes. She wanted to forget. Just forget. Just start over. That's all that Abolene wanted, was to forget that it had ever happened, that she had ever liked or thought about kissing Leon Jordan. Abolene just wanted to forget and she leaned back in the tub and answered her grandmother through the closed door, "I thought I was ready but I wasn't."

"Did he use a rubber?" China asked.

"No," Abolene whispered. "No."

Coyle

27

Coyle Redd sat on the porch swing smoking a cigarette. He had eaten the dinner that China had made for him, but he had not cleaned up. The dishes sat crusting with food on the dining-room table. What was left of the chicken was still on the platter with the faded gold trim and the faint pink roses in the middle. All of the creamed corn was gone and all of the rolls. A pitcher of tea sat sweating a ring into the polished mahogany.

Coyle Redd sat on the porch swing smoking a cigarette and watching the activities in the house across the street. He had seen Leon Jordan's car drive up too fast. He had seen the stiffness in Abolene's walk. He had watched China stand and lean against the newel post and walk down the steps towards her granddaughter. Coyle Redd had seen Abolene drop something into China's waiting palm.

The wind came up after China walked to the back of the house. It came up gentle enough at first, ruffling the picture of the Winnebago in Coyle's lap, fanning the embers of his cigarette so that it burned faster, cooling the hot August day enough to finally be pleasant.

August in Chatham County was a month known as

"dog days" and a breeze as cool as this one was a welcome change.

Coyle had kicked the porch swing into motion again and lit another cigarette. He took a sip from the tumbler of bourbon and ginger that sat on the porch rail. By the end of the month he would be gone.

Everything except the kitchen was ready for the auction. In his own room there was a stack of clothes piled into a corner, jeans and button-down shirts and socks. There was a pair of work boots and a pair of flip-flop sandals. There was a box with a fresh can of shaving cream, a fresh tube of toothpaste, an unopened toothbrush and razor and a hard, black Ace comb.

These were the things that Coyle would take with him when he left. Tomorrow he would go through the kitchen and pick out a few pots and pans, a few of the speckled enamelware plates and mugs, a few forks and knives and spoons. There would be time to do this tomorrow, to have it done by Monday when Mr. Jackson returned with his crew to go through the kitchen.

The breeze picked up and once again ruffled the picture that lay in Coyle's lap.

China had not come back from behind her house and Coyle assumed that she had gone inside through the back door. He wondered what it was that Abolene had given her. He wondered what it was that China had set down on the porch and then picked back up again before she stepped to the back of the house. He wondered where he would go when he left Chatham County.

Coyle looked down at the Winnebago. Everything a

man could possibly need was right there. A kitchen, a bed, a couch, a table, a bathroom. It was all right there, he had told China. A man doesn't need anything more than that.

The breeze suddenly turned to wind and picked the page out of Coyle's lap and blew it across the porch. He jumped up and ran after it, stomping it down with his foot. When he looked up, the unmowed grass in his yard was rippling like waves. The wind loosened a strand of Mamie's wisteria and banged it against the house. The wind blew a cloud of Chatham County dust off the driveway and across the yard and into Coyle's eyes.

He blinked against the stinging grit. The swing was creaking wildly on its chains. Coyle felt across the rail and found his drink and fought the wind across the porch, slamming the door hard against it.

It was cold. He could feel the goosebumps across his bare arms. He could feel a chill settling inside the house as if it was winter and the furnace was broken down. He felt his forehead for a fever. When he was able to open his eyes he went to the thermostat on the wall and checked the temperature. Fifty-five degrees, it said.

Coyle Redd turned the heat on in August.

The heat was turned up to ninety when the boys from the auction company found him on Monday morning. He was up in the attic. The slats in the vent had broken and were flung like sticks around the room. The neatly stacked and inventoried papers were lying everywhere. The door to the old Victrola had swung off one of its hinges. The picture of Bessie Redd, with her yellow auction tag, was lying in one of the scooped-out stair treads.

Coyle was wearing a red wool jacket and a yellow scarf. He was pinned beneath a fallen wardrobe that he had tried to push against the broken vent. The wardrobe had broken Coyle's neck and killed him instantly.

That wind had blown all across Chatham County. It had downed trees across three major highways. It had picked up chickens and given them to neighbors. It had turned over two outhouses and ripped the siding off a barn. It had whistled underneath the floorboards of China's house and caused Abolene to feel so cold that she got up in the middle of the night and crawled into bed with China.

China wrapped her arms around Abolene and listened to the wind rattle the windows in their frames.

"What if I'm pregnant?" Abolene had asked.

"Then we love it," China answered.

Abolene ran her hand across her belly. "I think I am," she said.

"I knew I was," China answered. "Walking to Roseberry from Cally's old cabin that morning, I knew I was pregnant."

The next day was quiet. The morning broke clear and beautiful, like the land had been scoured with a good hard rain. But there had been no rain that China could remember. Only wind.

She had lain awake and listened to it hurl around the edges of her house. She had gotten up and thrown another blanket across the bed and then climbed in and wrapped her arms around Abolene again.

In the morning she sat on the porch and drank a glass of iced tea. Things were quiet. China heard the creak of the screen door behind her.

"I'm going to the graveyard," Abolene told her, stepping out onto the porch.

"It's not Sunday," China said.

Abolene lay her hand on her stomach and said, "I'm going anyway."

China watched her walk down the lane, still moving a little stiffly. She watched her cross the highway and head into Roseberry's driveway.

Abolene passed by Roseberry as quietly as she could. She passed by it like someone was sleeping inside that she didn't want to wake. She crept by the dining room window and kept her head down. She stumbled into a laundry basket that had blown across the yard and she returned it to the back porch. When she did, she noticed the one strand of Mamie's wisteria that was hanging loosely from the rest. She noticed that the key to the back door had been ripped from its place on the light fixture and the string had wound itself around the thin branch of a maple tree.

Abolene left it there and walked along the gravel road that had been spread for Riley Redd's funeral. She walked past the tumbled-down logs of the cabins. She walked into the woods, along the old carriage trail, across the rushing brown waters of the Haw River and up the hill. Past the closed iron gates of the white Redds' cemetery. Past the spread of marble tombstones etched with dates and names and praying hands. Past the children's lambs and the stone bench and the over-grown boxwoods.

Abolene walked to the clearing in the woods and picked up the fallen sticks and swept the ground clean and sat, leaning against Cally's rock. Abolene lay her hand on her stomach and thought about the ache that she still felt between her legs. Abolene lay her hand on her stomach and thought about the small life that she knew was there.

"I'm not ready," she whispered. "I'm not ready."

A small breeze came up and whispered back to her. It stirred across her face and brushed at the ring and the button hanging against her throat. Abolene Redd reached up and touched her necklace and felt the breeze whisper across her skin. The breeze settled like warm hands across her shoulders. It was nothing like the wind of Friday night.

The wind of Friday night had been mentioned in that day's papers. It was before anyone knew that there had been damage beyond trees and outhouses and barns and a few scared chickens. It was before anyone knew that Coyle Redd had been killed by the wind of Friday night.

When Abolene came home from the graveyard, she sat on the top step of the porch and listened to China rocking in the old recliner behind her.

"It's too quiet," China said.

"What's it like to have a baby?" Abolene asked, her hand still resting on her stomach.

"It's magic," China replied. "It's pure magic."

"I got to go check on the earrings," Abolene said.

It was at the back of the house that Abolene found the

leather journal that had blown across the road on Friday night. It had blown out of the attic of Roseberry. It had scudded between the rows of oak trees and across the highway. It had scudded down the lane between the fields of cows taking shelter against a pile of rocks. It had scudded beneath China's house and it lay resting against the stones of the corner piling.

It lay closed when Abolene knelt in the dirt to reach under the house and check on the earrings. It lay closed and waiting and Abolene's fingers found it before they climbed the rocks to the crevice where the earrings were kept. The word "Records" was embossed across the front.

Abolene sat in the dirt and opened the old journal to pages of florid writing, to lists of names and dates and dollar amounts. Abolene opened the old leather journal and read, "Cleavis. Born to Cally. April, 1855. Sold. May 1861. $600."

China

28

On the day that Jackson's Auction Company found Coyle's body, China and Abolene were sitting outside. They watched as the young boys came bursting out of the house and milled restlessly about the porch. They watched as the police arrived, one squad car after another. They watched as an ambulance arrived and they watched as the body of Coyle Redd was carried down the wooden steps of Roseberry.

Abolene walked down the lane between the fields of cows. She crossed the highway and was stopped by a policeman asking if she had business there.

"We worked for him," Abolene said. "My grandmother and I. We worked for him and wondered what happened."

The officer told her. A freak accident, he said. That wind on Friday night, he said. It must have been strong here. It knocked a wardrobe over and caught Mr. Redd underneath.

Abolene nodded. She thanked the policeman and turned away and crossed the highway again. The press was arriving. Large vans with tall antennas were parked along the driveway, between the rows of oak trees. As Abolene was crossing the highway, a white man in a shiny gray car slowed down and yelled for her.

"Excuse me, girl," he said.

Abolene stopped.

"I'm looking for a different angle on this." He swept his arms towards Roseberry. "I hear there's some folks living close by that are descended from the slaves that worked this plantation. You know anything about that?"

"I hadn't heard that," Abolene said. "I hadn't heard anything about that." She rested one hand on her belly.

"I remember the day he was born," China said when Abolene told her what had happened to Coyle. "It was five weeks later that Riley tore the cabins down." China reached up and grabbed Abolene's arm. She sank her fingers into her skin and said, "That was Tom's bone-chilling sigh on Friday night. It killed the last of the white Redds and it brought us this."

China was sitting in the recliner with the old leather journal in her lap. She'd hardly let go of it since Abolene had found it.

Abolene nodded. She pulled an old slat-back chair up next to her grandmother and wrapped her arms around China's thin shoulders.

"You're shivering," Abolene said, pulling the worn yellow blanket across China's lap.

China lifted up the old journal and allowed Abolene to tuck the blanket around her legs. She settled the journal back in her lap and opened to the page with Cally's name.

They had found the names of Cleavis and Tom and Cally, and the names of Tuly and Jed and even Abe, although Abe had been born a free child. They found the names of house slaves and field hands alike. They found dollar amounts beside each and every name. They found dollar amounts beside the names of the people who had cleared the rocks out of the fields for plantings of cotton. They found dollar amounts beside the names of people who had cooked and cleaned inside of Roseberry long before China had followed her mother across the road.

They sat on the porch and watched a policeman wind yellow plastic tape around the porch of Roseberry. They watched the officer at the end of the driveway check press passes. They watched the edges of the highway fill up with onlookers. They watched people standing on the hoods of their cars, trying to see. They saw the ambulance leave with Coyle Redd's body.

"A man stopped me on the way back," Abolene said. "He was a reporter, looking for the descendants of Roseberry's slaves."

"What did you say?"

"I said I didn't know anything about it. You didn't want to talk to him, did you?"

"No," China said.

She looked down at the page in the journal. She touched her fingers to Cally's name and then she said, "I might have talked."

China turned the pages in the journal and touched the name of Cleavis, the name of Tom, the names of Tuly and Jed and Abe. China had gotten out of bed three times on Saturday night to open the old journal and run her fingers across the names.

Even before she knew that Coyle was dead, China had said to Abolene, "We're not giving this back."

"Why should we?" Abolene asked, standing in the kitchen with her hand on her stomach.

29

This was the story that began to claw inside the throat of China Redd. It eased her eyelids open in the mornings and floated its fingers across them at night. It settled on her shoulders like a featherless bird. It circled her house like wind.

It was the story of a woman named Cally, born with blue eyes and died with gray. It was the story of a boy named Cleavis who hauled water from a well but never got a bucket full to his mother. It was the story of a boy named William Lars Redd who slipped off a rock and drowned in the rushing brown waters of a river named Haw.

It was the story of Maude and Abe and Joe and Alfie and China Redd's own birth on the kitchen floor of a newly built house. It was the story of a man named Amzie Washington who used no words to talk his language to China Redd. It was the story of China, who wanted to know the things he had to say without them.

It was the story of Earnest, born with a stutter that only the birth of his own child could cure, and of Abolene, named for the earrings that Cally stole a long time ago on a moonless Carolina night.

It was the story of a man named Tom who struggled to keep his family together, who paced the dusty dirt of the horse barn on the nights that a man named Jennis visited Cally. Tom, who held the baby Cleavis in his arms and said, "You're more mine than his."

China wanted to tell of the bone-chilling sigh that escaped from Tom's lungs and how it circled Roseberry like wind and how, after he died, it came up out of the land, how it came up from the clearing of rocks up on the hill, how it came up from the piles of rocks in the fields, how it came up out of the well that William Lars Redd threw Cleavis's bucket of water back down into.

It was Tom's bone-chilling sigh that had finally ripped through the halls and rooms and attic of Roseberry. It was Tom's bone-chilling sigh that lifted the white Redds' family portraits off the staircase wall and flung them throughout the house. It was Tom's bone-chilling sigh that ran through the kitchen and ripped cabinet doors off their hinges and strewed pots and pans and dish towels across the floor, all the while leaving China's apron neatly folded and draped over the back of a chair. China Redd never doubted that it was Tom's bone-chilling sigh that felled the wardrobe across Coyle's back and took the last of the white Redds from the land called Roseberry.

No one knows the exact day that Mamie's wisteria broke through the dining room window of Roseberry and wound its way around the table legs that China had crawled on her hands and knees to polish. No one knows the exact date that Mamie's wisteria twisted itself around the light fixture and broke its frosted globe and curled itself around the sideboard and climbed the cracked plaster walls. No one knows the exact date that Mamie's wisteria crossed the table that China had served so many meals at and, twirling itself vine into vine, filled the room and trapped inside its weavings the crusty dishes of Coyle Redd's last meal.

No one knows the exact date but China Redd swears that it happened overnight. China Redd swears that Mamie's wisteria grew to be a thick, healthy vine inside of Roseberry on the very night that her great-grandchild was born.

China was sitting in the parlor with the old leather journal in her lap. She was sitting there, resting both hands on the pages of the journal, just as she used to rest her hands inside the cupped bowls of the attic stair treads. China was sitting there letting her hands rest and do no work, when she heard the sound of glass shattering from across the road and then the sound of Abolene calling for her.

Abolene lay in China's bed and just as she clutched her stomach and groaned with the pain of contractions China heard another groan coming from across the highway. Just as Abolene heard the first cries of her new baby, they both heard cries in the night air, all around them.

"What is it?" Abolene asked, barely raising her head from the pillow.

"It's a girl," China said.

"Outside. What is it outside?"

"It could be Tom again," China said. "It could be anybody. It could be Coyle." China cleared the baby's nose and throat and laid her across Abolene's stomach. "What will you name her?" she asked.

Abolene took her new baby in her arms and said, "Cally. I'm going to name her Cally."

When Abolene named her baby the world got quiet again.

It was the day that Cally was born that China felt her bones becoming tilted and dry and useless, like the tumbled-down logs of the cabins at the edge of the field. China felt her blood becoming thick and slow, like the silted waters of the Haw River. China felt like something was winding around her heart and choking it off, the same as Mamie's wisteria was winding around the edges of the dining room in the old Roseberry plantation. It was the day that Cally was born that China Redd felt like she was too tired to live anymore and began waiting to die.

Five weeks after Cally was born, Abolene carried her baby across the highway and down the driveway towards Roseberry. She came to the dining room window and saw Mamie's wisteria filling the inside of that room, saw its dark wood taking every inch of space. She held Cally up to the window and said, "Look," and she took the baby's hand and laid it on the vine and said, "It's not going to get cut back anymore. You know that, Cally? It's going to grow."

Across the road, China was easing herself into the old recliner on the porch. She pulled the thin yellow blanket across her legs and rested her hands on the leather journal in her lap. She eased her head back and closed her eyes and whispered to the breeze, "Maybe today."